# AMY AND LAURA

### by MARILYN SACHS

Cover illustration by Ruth Sanderson

SCHOLASTIC BOOK SERVICES
New York Toronto London Auckland Sydney Tokyo

*Books by Marilyn Sachs*
*available through Scholastic Book Services*

Amy Moves In
Amy and Laura
Laura's Luck

*For my daughter Anne*
*and my son Paul*

ISBN 0-590-32299-0

12 11 10 9 8 7 6 5 4 3 2 1      11      1 2 3 4 5 6/8

Printed in the U.S.A.                    01

# Contents

# Amy

Amy was ten. Today, October 24, she became ten and a half.

"Some families," she told Aunt Minnie, "have a half a cake when a person becomes something and a half."

"Go away, I'm busy," said Aunt Minnie.

"Come here, Amy," Laura said, a glint in her eye. She grabbed Amy and gave her five smacks.

"What are you hitting me for?" Amy howled.

"I'm ·celebrating your half-birthday," Laura explained. "So that's why I gave you five smacks. Actually, I should give you a quarter of a smack too, since that's half of a half."

"I hate you," Amy said, and ran off.

She told Cynthia about it on the way to school that morning, and Cynthia said she was glad she didn't have an older sister.

"It's bad enough having a kid brother," she said, "but at least he doesn't pick on me and boss me around all the time the way your sister does."

Amy knew that Cynthia didn't like Laura very much, and today she shared her friend's feelings completely. She continued grumbling about Laura, until Cynthia finally said, "Anyway — what are you wearing to the party?"

"What party?"

"Helen Prendergast's party. Her Halloween party. I'm going dressed up like a tramp."

Amy walked along silently.

"What are you wearing?" Cynthia repeated.

"Oh," Amy tried to appear unconcerned. "I'm not going."

"Why not?"

Amy stopped walking. "I'm not going," she said sullenly, "because she didn't ask me."

Cynthia's eyes opened wide in surprise. "Are you sure? She asked just about every other girl in the class. Annette is going, and Bernice, and Rhoda, and Gladys, and — "

"Well, she didn't ask me," Amy shouted.

"Maybe she forgot," Cynthia suggested.

A hopeful feeling grew inside Amy. "Maybe she did," she said. "I'll ask her."

The bell hadn't rung when they reached the schoolyard, so Amy began looking for Helen. There she was, playing Follow the

Leader with Bernice and some other girls. Amy hurried over to her.

"Hi, Helen," she said pleasantly.

"Oh — hi," Helen answered, jumping over an assortment of books on the ground, and following the other players as they wove in and out between the books.

"Uh — Helen," Amy continued, "can I see you for a minute?"

Helen stopped jumping and looked at her. "What do you want?" she asked.

"In private," Amy explained.

She led Helen over to an unoccupied corner of the yard.

"What is it?" said Helen.

Amy put her books on the ground between her legs and looked at Helen's feet.

"Cynthia told me you're having a Halloween party," she said, and waited.

"That's right," Helen answered, and waited.

"Well, I just wondered," Amy continued, looking at her own feet now, "I mean, I understand most of the girls in the class are going, and I just wondered — well —" (oh, how she hated Helen!) — "I wondered if you forgot to ask me." She took a deep breath, and looked right up at Helen.

There was a serious frown on Helen's

face, so Amy looked down at her own feet again.

"No," Helen said, "I didn't forget."

"Well," Amy said sadly, "I don't know why you're not inviting me. I always liked you very much, and I thought you liked me." She shifted her gaze to the hole in her glove.

"I like you all right," Helen said, "but you didn't invite me to your birthday party, so why should I invite you to my Halloween party?"

"I didn't invite you to my birthday party," Amy explained patiently, "because I didn't know you very well then. I mean, I always liked you but I just didn't know you very well then. I've really gotten to know you real well since then, though." Amy looked intently at her finger pushing its way back and forth through the hole in the glove.

Helen was silent. Amy shoved her books with her foot and said softly, "This year, though, I'll definitely invite you to my birthday party. If you invite me to your Halloween party, I swear I will."

"You invited Bernice Rogers," Helen went on in a strained voice, "my best friend, and you knew she was my best friend, but you didn't invite me."

"I didn't know," Amy protested, looking straight into Helen's eyes. "Honestly, I didn't

4

know. But this year, I promise, I'll invite you and I won't invite her."

Helen's face began to lose its grim look.

"Come on, Helen," Amy said sweetly, "don't be like that."

"All right," Helen said finally. "You swear you'll invite me to your party?"

Amy kissed two fingers up to heaven. "I swear," she said solemnly.

"Then you can come to mine." Helen smiled.

Amy picked up her books, crooked her arm through Helen's, and together they walked back to the other girls. "Well, it was worth it," Amy thought. She really didn't care that much for Helen, and ordinarily wouldn't have considered inviting her to the birthday party. But that's the way it was. She had never been to a Halloween party in her whole life, and her own birthday party wouldn't take place until April anyway.

Just as the bell rang, she saw Rosa, waved to her, and together they hurried over to their line.

"Can you come over today?" Rosa asked.

"Not today," Amy said. "My mother's definitely coming home from the hospital tomorrow, and we have lots of things to do today getting ready."

"I'm glad she's finally coming home," said

Rosa. "It's no good when your mother's not home."

"And it's nearly a year since the accident," Amy whispered out of the corner of her mouth, as silence began to descend on the schoolyard. "Rosa, you should see the drapes my aunt made! Maybe you can come over Monday and see them, and meet my mother. You never met her, but I told her about you in the letters I wrote her, and . . ."

Uh-uh, a monitor was headed in her direction. Amy stood stiffly in her place, and began licking her lips as if she hadn't really been talking at all — just airing her mouth a little.

"Can't you ever stop talking?" snapped the monitor, stopping right next to Amy.

"Who, me?" Amy asked innocently. The monitor was that big mean-looking one in 8B. Everybody hated her.

"I ought to pull you out of line," the monitor continued.

"Please," Rosa broke in, "it was my fault. I asked her a question, and she was only answering it."

"Well, you know you're not supposed to talk in line," the monitor said to Rosa in not quite such a mean voice.

"Yes, I'm very sorry," Rosa said, really looking very sorry.

The monitor moved away. Amy smiled lovingly at Rosa, and the lines started moving into the building. Winding its way up the staircase, past the watchful monitors who stood on each landing, Amy's line emerged from the staircase on the third floor and came to a halt outside Room 312. The sign on the door said 5B[1], and Mrs. Malucci, the teacher, stood in the hall talking to Miss Langendorf. The children stood wiggling patiently until Mrs. Malucci decided to notice them. She was talking very earnestly to Miss Langendorf, stooping forward a little, since Miss Langendorf was nearly a head shorter than she was. Miss Langendorf wasn't saying anything, just shaking her head back and forth in sympathetic understanding of whatever it was Mrs. Malucci was telling her, and occasionally making "tsk, tsk, tsk" noises with her tongue.

None of the children spoke. Amy shifted her weight over to her left foot, and some of the other children moved themselves into more comfortable standing positions. Finally Mrs. Malucci looked up. "Stop it!" she said, and turned her attention back to Miss Langendorf.

Mrs. Malucci's morning greeting to her class seldom varied. Usually, she said, "Stop it!" Sometimes, she said, "Be quiet there!"

She was by far the most unpleasant teacher Amy had ever had. Why, compared to Mrs. Malucci, Amy's last teacher, Miss Parker, seemed absolutely lovable. Miss Parker used to smile sometimes. Occasionally she even laughed. And if she didn't like all the children in her class, at least she did have a number of favorites. Mrs. Malucci seldom smiled. Occasionally, at three o'clock, when the children, coated and hatted, prepared to march off down the stairs and home, the corners of Mrs. Malucci's lips might rise quickly as she said, "Good-bye, good-bye." And as for favorites, well, even Annette de Luca, who was always teacher's pet, couldn't make a dent. Of course, that was one thing you had to admit: Mrs. Malucci was fair. She didn't like anybody.

Miss Langendorf's class finally hove into sight, and with a final "tsk, tsk" Miss Langendorf turned away from Mrs. Malucci. She smiled at the children in her class, said, "Well, hello again," and turned with them into Room 310.

Mrs. Malucci motioned with her head, and her class silently passed before her into its room.

"Bernard," Amy heard Mrs. Malucci say to a boy in front of the line, "use your handkerchief! That's what it's for."

8

As Amy passed in front of her teacher, she looked up into Mrs. Malucci's gray, watery eyes that always made her feel as if her own eyes were wet and, as she did every morning, smiled a sweet, hopeful smile. Mrs. Malucci's head moved downward ever so slightly in acknowledgment, and that was all. Amy sighed. She wished Mrs. Malucci liked her. She wished she could like Mrs. Malucci. It was never comfortable not liking people.

After the children had hung up their clothing, they sat down silently in their seats and clasped their hands together on top of their desks. Mrs. Malucci always liked to have the children's hands plainly in sight at all times.

"Pass your homework forward," Mrs. Malucci commanded.

Amy bent down low under her desk as she fished her homework out from her notebook. Protected by the rustling of papers all around her, she whispered, "Hey, Rosa," to her friend who sat in the seat next to hers. Rosa looked toward her, and Amy motioned with her head toward the front of the room where Mrs. Malucci stood, crossed her eyes, and made the funniest face she could. Rosa's face turned crimson as she held back the explosive giggle, and quickly turned away from Amy. Rosa was always such a good girl, so respectful of teachers.

"John Muller," Mrs. Malucci was saying, "do you have a note from your mother explaining your absence Monday?"

"Oh," groaned the boy, "I forgot again."

"Stand up, John, when you speak to me," said Mrs. Malucci.

"Okay," said John rising.

"What was that?" said Mrs. Malucci.

"I mean — yes, Mrs. Malucci," said John.

"Now, John," Mrs. Malucci said slowly, "I have asked you for that note three times. If it is not in by tomorrow, I will have the truant officer go around to your house and talk to your mother. Do you understand?"

"Yes," whispered John.

"Yes what?"

"Yes, Mrs. Malucci."

"Sit down, John."

John sat down, and Mrs. Malucci began handing out sheets of yellow paper. Another composition! Amy nearly groaned out loud.

"Now today," Mrs. Malucci said, "I want you all to write a composition on — let me see — on 'My Best Friend.' I hope it will be a better set of papers than the ones you did on Tuesday." Mrs. Malucci looked around the classroom in disgust. "It seems to me that there are very few children in this class who realize that there are other marks of punctuation in the English language besides the period." She looked right at Amy. "Amy Stern," she said, "can you tell the class some other punctuation marks?"

"Yes, Mrs. Malucci," Amy said rising, and smiling. This was easy. "There is the question mark, the comma, the apostrophe, and, uh — "

"Yes," said Mrs. Malucci, "and not one of those you mentioned appeared on your last composition. Yours was the worst in that respect." A relieved titter broke from the class, and Amy bit her lip. "Although," Mrs. Malucci continued mercilessly, looking around the room and quelling the happy sound, "I wasn't satisfied with anybody else's paper either. Now start working, and try to think about what you're doing for a change."

Amy sat down feeling disgraced and abandoned. Why was it people always said married teachers who had children of their own understood children better than single teachers? Mrs. Malucci was married. It was said she even had five children, possibly six. So why didn't she understand children? Why did she always say mean things to children, in front of the whole class too? Amy remembered the composition she had written on Tuesday very well. The subject was "A Funny Story," and she had written such a funny story, such a *long*, funny story too.

11

Why, she had even needed two sheets of paper, and she had nearly laughed out loud as she was writing it. She had been positive Mrs. Malucci would think it was wonderful, but no, count on Mrs. Malucci always to find something nasty to say.

She heard a very faint tapping on the desk next to hers and turned to meet Rosa's sympathetic face. Rosa smiled encouragingly, carefully pointed with her pencil to the paper on her desk, and then, with the pencil, pointed toward Amy. A great happiness rose in Amy's chest. Rosa meant that she was going to say on her paper that Amy Stern was her best friend.

Well! Amy took up her own pencil and settled herself over the empty paper on her desk. "My Best Friend — Rosa Ferrara," she thought in her mind.

"Please, Mrs. Malucci," came a voice from the back, "can I sharpen my pencil?"

"*May* I sharpen my pencil, Henry," corrected Mrs. Malucci. "Come on, then!"

Everybody watched as Henry clumped to the front of the room, ground his pencil in the sharpener, and clumped back to his seat. Then, slowly, the rows of backs bent over the rows of papers on desks.

"Rosa Ferrara has the most beautiful black braids in the world," Amy thought to herself, pushing her pencil through her own despised blond, frizzy curls. Her blue eyes narrowed on the empty paper as she prepared to fill it with words.

"Mrs. Malucci, *may* I please sharpen my pencil too?"

All thinking about "My Best Friend" halted as forty-three pairs of eyes settled on Mrs. Malucci's face.

"Come, come!" said Mrs. Malucci irritably, "and if anybody else needs to sharpen his pencil, he had better do it right now."

Cynthia marched to the front of the classroom, and a few other children followed. The whirring of the sharpener began again, stopped, and began again. As Cynthia passed Amy's desk on her way back to her seat, she stuck out her tongue and pointed right at Amy with her pencil and then at the empty sheet of paper on Amy's desk.

Well! Was Cynthia actually going to write that she, Amy, was her best friend? And all the time she had supposed that Cynthia considered Annette de Luca her best friend. Of course, for the past two weeks Cynthia and Annette had been mad at each other and weren't even talking. But still! Amy glowed with contentment.

And then the horror of her predicament struck her. Desperately she glued her eyes

13

on the last of the pencil sharpeners, watched him as he returned to his seat, saw the rhythmic lines of backs bent over their work, and her skinny little face wrinkled with her problem.

Who was her best friend anyway? Was it Cynthia or was it Rosa? She wished somebody would tell her. If only Laura were here! But then, she knew very well Laura's opinion on the subject. Laura couldn't stand Cynthia and considered her a bad influence on Amy. Which was sort of a compliment, since it meant that Laura felt there was somebody in the world worse than Amy. Generally, Laura didn't approve of any of Amy's friends. But she did like Rosa. "A nice, quiet little girl with good manners," she said.

Amy liked Rosa too, but not because she was a nice, quiet little girl with good manners. She liked her because she was fun to be with in spite of her good manners and quiet ways. Rosa was especially fun to be with on cold or rainy days when they played indoors. If they played at Rosa's house, which Amy preferred, they could dress up in the beautiful clothes that Rosa's family used to wear when they lived in Puerto Rico. Then, if nobody was in the living room, they could turn on the radio and hunt for some appropriate music. Sad music was best, because they liked to act out sad stories. Rosa was such a magnificent actress that she always carried Amy breathlessly along with her into the story they were acting. Like the time Rosa played the part of a mother whose child was very sick, and Amy was the nurse. The child had suddenly taken a turn for the worse.

"I'm sorry," Amy said sadly, handing back the doll, wrapped in a blanket. "We've done everything we could for him. It's too late."

On that day the music had been especially suitable. Just as Amy spoke, a low beating of drums began.

Rosa's trembling hands reached for the child. She pressed her lips to its cold forehead and dropped to her knees. Back and forth she rocked, crooning to it in Spanish.

"You have other children," Amy said solemnly. "They need you."

But the grief-stricken figure at her feet crouched over the child, kissing it and pleading with it to come back.

There was a lump in Amy's throat as she knelt beside Rosa, and implored her, "Be brave!"

Then the moaning started, low and broken, as the mother rocked backward and forward, the dead child in her arms, and tears, real tears, flowing down her cheeks.

Amy gasped, and began sobbing herself. And the two of them huddled over the poor lost baby, weeping uncontrollably until the music stopped and the commercial began.

If they played at Amy's house, which Rosa preferred, they generally crayoned, or played Chinese Checkers or Monopoly. And because Laura held such a high opinion of Rosa, sometimes she might even condescend to play with them if she had nothing better to do. And the afternoon would pass quietly and pleasantly.

But on fine days, something inside Amy hungered for Cynthia. Nobody could rollerskate so swiftly and so noisily as Cynthia. Nobody could dream up such dangerous expeditions as Cynthia. And nobody could fight so well or talk so fresh as Cynthia.

Amy nibbled on her pencil, and suddenly became aware of Mrs. Malucci's eyes on her. Quickly she crouched low over her desk, hiding behind the back in front of her. Out of the corner of her eye, she watched Rosa turn the paper on her desk and begin writing on the other side.

Jerry Kerner held up his hand for another sheet of paper. Amy looked at the empty paper on her own desk and felt like crying. She just could not decide. And if she did decide on one or the other, what would she do when the other one, the one she had not chosen, asked her what she had written?

"Just start writing," she told herself. "Write anything." But her pencil poised motionlessly above the paper. "Rosa, write Rosa!" she said to herself. "You know she's really your best friend — not just when she's mad at somebody, but all the time." And it was true. Rosa never made fun of her the way Cynthia often did. Never said she was a coward or skinny or disgusting. Rosa never pushed her around or whispered secrets in somebody else's ear about her. "Write Rosa!" she said to herself.

But there were other thoughts too: of high adventure in Crotona Park, of the glory when she followed after Cynthia in scaling Indian Rock and driving off their foes, of the feel of her palm stinging when Cynthia played handball with her in the schoolyard, of the joy when Cynthia whispered in her ear about somebody else.

Rosa put her pencil down, leaned back in her seat, and smiled over at Amy. All around her, Amy could hear the rustling sound of children finished with their work.

"I have to write something — anything," she thought desperately. "I know, I know. I won't write about either of them." Frantically she began.

A long time ago, before I lived here, I lived in another neighborhood, and my best friend there was a girl named Celia Gerber.

"All right, class," said Mrs. Malucci, "pass your papers forward."

Later that afternoon, Amy stood outside the school waiting for Laura. In her notebook was an empty sheet of paper on which she was to bring back tomorrow a "decent" composition about "My Best Friend." Mrs. Malucci had made some other remarks about people who are lazy, and people who daydream, and people who don't follow instructions. Amy was reviewing these different comments in her mind, and thinking that Mrs. Malucci was not really fair at all. Maybe she didn't have favorites, but Amy was beginning to feel that whatever was the opposite of favorite, she, Amy Stern, filled that position in Mrs. Malucci's heart. "She's always picking on me," she grumbled, kicking at a crack in the pavement.

Anyway, thank goodness, she didn't have to walk home with Cynthia and talk about their compositions. Usually she walked to and from school with Cynthia, since Rosa lived in another direction, but today she had agreed to wait for Laura and help carry home her diorama of *The Hunchback of Notre Dame*.

Amy watched as the children from Laura's class began to come through the door. Roslyn Beckerman waved at her.

"Amy!"

"Yes?"

"Laura says not to wait. She had to stay in, so she says you should go home. She'll leave the diorama in school till tomorrow."

"What did she do?" Amy asked.

"Nothing." Roslyn laughed. "When does your sister ever get in trouble? Mrs. Foster just wanted to talk to her about something. I don't know what."

Amy waited around a little longer anyway. She hated walking home by herself. But after a while, nobody else came through the doors, and the schoolyard began emptying out. Slowly, looking over her shoulder every so often, she began walking home. She really wished Laura could have been with her. Even though she knew what Laura would say, she just needed to have somebody to talk to about her composition and Mrs. Malucci.

One more backward glance as she left the schoolyard, and then Amy began hurrying. She really shouldn't dawdle today. Aunt

Minnie had so many jobs for her to do. And then, tomorrow! Oh, she couldn't wait for tomorrow! Mama was coming home. Mama. Mama. Mama. What would Mama think of Mrs. Malucci? Amy wondered. What would she advise her to do about "My Best Friend"? She tried to concentrate on Mama's face, but it was not very distinct in her mind. She crossed Boston Road, hurried past the bakery and the five and dime store, and waited as a car passed to cross the last street that separated her from her block.

On Amy's block, all of the houses were apartment houses, and all looked exactly the same. Made of red brick, five stories high, with gray-white stoops in front, they stretched from one end of the street to the other.

Henry, Cynthia's little brother, was sitting on the stoop of the first house, and as Amy passed he began chanting:

> Fat and Skinny ran a race.
> Skinny fell down and broke her face.
> And Fat won the race.

Amy just ignored him and kept on walking. At the second house from the corner, she turned, walked slowly onto her own stoop, through the outside door, and into the vestibule. In front of the wall of shiny letter boxes, Amy paused a moment and reflected.

Should she tell Aunt Minnie about the composition? No, Aunt Minnie was too busy. Why did Laura have to stay in anyway? And what was she going to do about getting the composition written by tomorrow? Wasn't there anybody who could help her? A hopeless, gloomy feeling enveloped her as she ran up the stairs to the first landing, opened the door marked 1A, and walked in.

Framed by the new peacock-blue drapes at the window, Mama sat by herself in the living room in the wheel chair Daddy had brought home for her yesterday. She leaned forward, smiling, as Amy came into the room. "Amy!" she said.

Amy didn't stop moving until she was sitting in Mama's lap in the wheel chair and Mama's arms were tight around her. Above her, Mama's familiar face was smiling at her, and she nuzzled her cheek against Mama's. In the back of her mind were a million questions: How did Mama get here? Why was she here today instead of tomorrow? What was that thing on her leg? But there was no time for any questions.

Happier than she had been all day, Amy began telling Mama all about Mrs. Malucci and "My Best Friend."

Laura felt like singing. Actually, she felt like singing and dancing too. And as she hurried out the door into the empty schoolyard, she did skip two or three gay little skips before she thought to look around and see if anybody was watching.

She knew that tomorrow, when Mama came home, she would be even happier than today, and yet it seemed impossible that any further joy could be crammed into her.

Her hand moved slowly and deliciously into her coat pocket, and she let her fingers explore a sleek, pointed surface. Just one more look, and then she'd hurry home and break the good news to Amy and Aunt Minnie. She pulled it out of her pocket, cradling it lovingly in her hand, and examined its glistening beauty. The five-pointed star had written across its surface, first "P.S. 63," and then, under it, MONITOR.

Just think: it was hers to wear until she graduated! That meant she would have it this term — 7B — next term — 8A — and the next — 8B. A whole year and a half. She was twelve years old now, and she would be thirteen and a half when she had to give it up — certainly a long, long way off. Tomorrow morning, she would report to Stuart Johnson, the head monitor, for her assignment. She would have to arrive at school at eight thirty, fifteen minutes earlier than the other children. And then, after that, she could pin the star on her coat, and she would be a monitor. Trembling with excitement, Laura stood silently looking at the lovely star. What an honor it was to be chosen! Her full cheeks flushed with pleasure, her brown eyes sparkled.

Laura was tall for her age, and not at all pretty. At least, she had never considered herself pretty. She weighed more than she should, clumped heavily when she walked, had straight, lanky brown hair, and two big front teeth that stuck out. Ever since July she had worn braces, and sometimes when she examined her face in the mirror, it did seem as if her teeth had begun to recede. But most of the time her appearance seemed changeless. An interesting face — yes, she believed this was true — not pretty certainly, but interesting — yes. Her sister, Amy, was pretty, although she certainly wasn't going to tell Amy she thought so. The brat was vain enough as it was. Those big, fluffy curls she had! Her blue eyes and rosy cheeks! And her even, straight teeth! Sometimes when Amy was asleep, Laura would gaze lovingly at that still, smooth little face and feel almost as if there was nothing in the world she wouldn't do for her little sister. But when Amy was awake, and that big mouth of hers went on and on about all sorts of nonsensical things, then Laura couldn't stand her.

Actually, she was even proud of Amy's pretty face. God had arranged things rather neatly, she thought. He had given Amy the beauty and Laura the brains. Usually Laura felt she was luckier than Amy, since beauty fades but a good mind endures. This thought made it all the more possible for Laura to cope with Amy's beauty.

Laura slid her hand back into her pocket and kept it there, gently touching her star. She began walking, and thinking again as she walked about how it had all come to pass. "No, no, start at the beginning," she ordered those delightful thoughts that came rushing into her mind all at the same time.

The day had started almost like any other day. Almost, but not quite. Because this was the day before Mama came home, so it was a special day, and Laura felt happy to begin with. Breakfast had been somewhat scantier than usual, since Aunt Minnie had so many odds and ends to tie up. Laura sliced a banana into her bowl of cold cereal, sprinkled raisins and brown sugar on top, and poured milk over the whole thing. She helped herself to two pieces of toast with jelly and drank a glass and a half of milk.

"Do you want an orange, Laura?" suggested Aunt Minnie.

"Okay." Laura began peeling her orange, and watched Amy looking in disgust at her uneaten bowl of cereal.

"What's the matter, Amy?" Aunt Minnie said, trying to sound patient.

Amy pushed away her bowl. "I don't like cornflakes," she said. "I like French toast."

"I don't have time this morning to make you French toast," Aunt Minnie said, the patience fading in her voice. "Come on and eat your cereal now."

"I like pancakes too," Amy continued sullenly.

"I don't have time to make you pancakes either this morning!" screamed Aunt Minnie.

"I'm not hungry," Amy said, shrugging her shoulders and rising from the table. "I'm not eating anything."

Amy's picky eating habits were a source of great concern to grownups. Even Aunt Minnie, who was always busy, gave up some of her valuable time every day to prepare special dishes to tempt Amy's uncertain appetite.

"You're a selfish brat," Laura said pleasantly, peeling the white inside skin from her orange. "Mama's coming home tomorrow, and nobody has time to fuss over you. So sit down and eat your breakfast like a good little girl, or you can starve to death."

Amy pushed her chair back with great dignity and walked out of the room, her nose in the air.

"I'll make her French toast," Aunt Minnie sighed. "She's got to eat something."

"I don't think you should bother," said Laura, "but I'll have a piece too."

Well fortified, Laura had arrived in school looking forward to another interesting day. Today was Thursday, and on Thursday they had nature study. Mr. Gray, the nature-study teacher, let them feed and handle the white mice and the baby guinea pigs. Since Laura had been to camp during the summer and had learned so much about trees and flowers, she had prepared such an impressive nature scrapbook that Mr. Gray had asked her if he could keep it for a while to show to the students. He had also asked her if she would like to spend her Monday-morning recess in the nature room as his assistant.

Today was also the day they were taking home their dioramas. Laura had been so concerned that Mrs. Foster would want to keep the dioramas another week. She just felt hers should be home when Mama arrived. Mama would certainly be amazed. Even Mrs. Foster, who liked all the dioramas, had admitted to the class, "Laura's is certainly the most unusual."

Laura was not surprised that Mrs. Foster should say so. She had spent days and days working on the diorama, and although usually her art work was not considered outstanding, the diorama was the crowning glory of her whole life. She expected that she would keep it forever.

It was in the inside of a cardboard box, sitting on its side. Laura had painted a gray sky above with black, ominous clouds. And painfully and carefully, she had traced a picture of Notre Dame Cathedral onto another piece of cardboard, which she glued into the center of the box. She had painted the stones of the cathedral a lighter gray than the sky, with dull blue patches here and there. Out of one of the windows appeared the beautiful head of Esmeralda, the unfortunate little gypsy girl. She had painted the face and that part of the dress that showed in brilliant colors, so that it was the only bright spot in the

27

whole scene. Down on the ground, she had painted long, dark shadows above mud-colored cobblestones. And moving through the shadows, on another piece of cardboard, was the pathetic, twisted shape of Quasimodo, the hunchback of Notre Dame.

It had turned out so magnificently that even Aunt Minnie had taken a deep breath when she saw it and exclaimed, "Who would have thought of such a thing?"

But as it turned out, the day held even greater pleasures in store. Her spelling-test paper was returned to her with 100 scrawled across the top in red pencil; Mrs. Foster had asked her to go over $R \times T \times P = 1$ with Jack Lazarus, who had been absent earlier in the week. Jack was such a nice, intelligent boy, even if his ears did stick out on either side of his bony face. In between talking about $R \times T \times P = 1$, Jack had offered to show her his stamp album, which had won second prize in an after-school stamp tournament. He offered to bring it over to her house this afternoon, but she told him about Mama coming home tomorrow; so he said he could come any afternoon next week she liked. He really seemed anxious to show her the album, and it gave her a warm, bubbly feeling thinking about him. You didn't even notice his ears once you got to know him.

But capping off the whole day was what happened as the children in Laura's class rose at three o'clock to get their hats and coats and go home.

"Laura," Mrs. Foster said, smiling, so Laura knew nothing was wrong, "please stay after the others leave."

When they were alone, Mrs. Foster said, "Laura, how would you like to be a monitor?"

"A monitor?" Laura repeated blankly.

"Yes," explained Mrs. Foster. "There is one vacancy on the squad, and Mr. De Silva asked me if there was anybody in my class who might make a good monitor. He says the person must be a good student, trustworthy, and dependable. You would have to come to school fifteen minutes earlier in the morning and leave probably fifteen minutes later in the afternoon."

Laura stood there thinking. It was all so unexpected, she hardly knew what to think.

"Of course," continued Mrs. Foster, "if you'd rather not take on the job, you don't have to. I imagine there are a number of other children in the class who would be eager to join the squad."

"Oh, it isn't that," Laura said slowly. "I don't know . . . Do you think I would be good at it?"

"Yes I do." Mrs. Foster smiled. "That's why I asked you first."

Laura licked her braces reflectively as the excitement began mounting inside her. "Yes," she said, "I think I'd like to try."

"Good!" said Mrs. Foster. "Go on down to the gym and see Mr. De Silva. He'll tell you what you need to do." She walked back to her desk and began arranging her papers. "I don't suppose your mother will object, will she? You'll need her permission."

"Oh no," Laura said, and then looked down at her feet as she explained slowly, "my mother's coming home from the hospital tomorrow."

"Hospital!" Mrs. Foster looked up from her desk. "I hope it's nothing serious."

"She's been away since last December," Laura continued. "She was hit by a car. I haven't seen her since then." Laura took a deep breath, and looked up at Mrs. Foster. "There's a wheel chair my father brought home. He says until she's stronger . . . I don't know . . . I haven't seen her."

"Oh, Laura!" Mrs. Foster left her desk and put her arms on Laura's shoulders. "I didn't know."

"But she's coming home tomorrow," Laura went on, trying to shape her quivering lips into a smile, "so she must be much better."

Mrs. Foster nodded, and patted Laura's shoulder. "Of course she is, of course. And I can just imagine how much she's looking forward to being with you again. She's a very lucky woman to have a daughter like you."

"My mother . . ." Laura began, but her voice drifted away. Even to somebody as good and sympathetic as Mrs. Foster, it was impossible for Laura to tell just what her mother was and what she meant to her. Everybody had a mother, naturally, but nobody that she knew had a mother like hers. She and Mama had always been so close, like friends almost. There was nothing she couldn't talk to Mama about, and nothing that Mama didn't understand. Of course Amy loved Mama too, but not the way she did. And of course Mama loved Amy. Sometimes Laura was jealous of just how much Mama loved Amy. And yet there was something special between Laura and Mama, something different from what was between Amy and Mama. Maybe it was because she and Mama were so much alike and thought the same way about most things. Amy acted more like most children do with their mothers, sometimes good, sometimes bad. Often Mama had to punish her, but it was very seldom that she had to punish Laura. And even then, it was usually over Amy, and not because Laura had been disobedient or fresh to her.

"Mama likes you better than me," Amy sometimes grumbled.

But Laura didn't really believe this was so, even though she would have liked to. But she was certain that she loved Mama better than Amy. It was obvious. After the accident, when Aunt Minnie came to take care of them. Amy, after blubbering for a day or two, had resumed activities almost as if it made no difference whether or not Mama was home. It was almost shocking the way she even sat on Aunt Minnie's lap and jabbered to her the way she did with Mama, nuzzling Aunt Minnie's cheek with her own in the same way.

For Laura, everything had turned topsy-turvy without Mama. She had managed to get along with Aunt Minnie, but nothing was right. Nothing was comfortable. The long, lonely months had passed somehow, but she had been waiting all along for Mama to return and make it all the way it used to be.

"I'd better go," Laura finally said, but stayed where she was, enjoying the feel of Mrs. Foster's arms on her shoulders. "We have a lot to do today. My aunt wants me to help her get everything ready for tomorrow.

That's my Aunt Minnie, I mean. She's been taking care of us since — since the accident."

Mrs. Foster nodded.

Aunt Minnie had been cleaning the house for the past few weeks with an even greater fury than usual. Everything gleamed and glistened with soap and polish. And then, last night —

"My aunt made drapes for the living room," Laura said shyly to Mrs. Foster. "She bought the material at a fire sale from Drexler's Dry Goods Store on Bathgate Avenue."

She looked wonderingly at her teacher. Did Mrs. Foster know anything about fire sales and the bargains on Bathgate Avenue? But Mrs. Foster smiled encouragingly, so Laura continued. "We never had drapes before. They're blue — peacock blue, my aunt says — and so beautiful! Last night, my father put them up." Laura nearly began laughing as she thought of Daddy, struggling in the heavy folds and saying the kind of things one doesn't repeat to teachers.

"I can imagine how beautiful they are, Mrs. Foster murmured. "Won't your mother be pleased when she sees them!"

"Oh yes," Laura cried, suddenly radiant and bubblng with talk now. "And my aunt's going to make a marble cake today, and buy a duck. We wanted her to make a turkey, but she says she can't get a decent turkey until Thanksgiving."

"Oh?" said Mrs. Foster.

"And I'm going to wrap up a pink fascinator I knit for my mother in fancy paper, and clean all the drawers in my chest of drawers," Laura went on breathlessly, "and, oh — I wanted to take my diorama home today, but — well — I can still take it home tomorrow, and — oh — I better hurry."

Mrs. Foster laughed. "Don't forget to see Mr. De Silva. I'm sure he won't keep you long."

"Yes, I will." Laura grabbed her coat and hurried to the door. Then she stopped for a moment, turned, and smiled awkwardly at her teacher. "Thank you, Mrs. Foster," she said. "I never thought about being a monitor before, but now I don't know why I never did. I know my mother will be pleased too."

And now she was hurrying home, the star in her pocket and happiness tingling inside her. Up the stairs to the house she went, through the door, and stopped. There were people in the living room. Daddy — home from work at this time? Aunt Minnie . . . Amy . . . and in the wheel chair in front of the drapes, sat . . . a woman.

"Laura!" said the woman. It was Mama. But it wasn't Mama either. The woman in the chair was heavy, and her hair was full of gray. And on one leg was a clumsy steel brace. "No, no, no!" thought Laura. "Not like this!" The picture of Mama she had carried with her all this long time — young, slim, with shining brown hair, remained stubbornly in her mind as she blinked at the waiting figure in the wheel chair.

"Yes, it's true, Laura," Daddy was saying happily. "Mama's home. She really is. The doctor called me at work this morning and said she could go home today. Laura!"

For Laura had turned and run sobbing down the long hall — away from Mama.

"What's the matter with you?" Daddy hissed as he followed Laura into the kitchen, closing the door behind him.

Laura looked up into Daddy's angry face, but she was crying so hard she couldn't say a word.

"What a way to behave — on her first day home, too. How do you think she feels seeing you carry on like this?" Daddy continued in a furious whisper.

Her shoulders heaving with sobs, Laura flopped into a chair, laid her head down on the kitchen table, and cried.

After a minute, Daddy's hand began patting her shoulder. "Laura! Don't, Laura!" he said slowly.

"Oh, Daddy," she cried, "she's so . . . so . . . I thought she was all better."

"Shh, shh," Daddy whispered, sitting down next to her. "She'll hear you."

Laura went on crying, and for a few moments there was only the sound of her sobs. Then Daddy said softly, "Look, Laura, you have to stop crying. For her sake, you just *have* to stop."

Laura tried, choking back the misery, and making little gasping noises.

"That's better," Daddy said, patting her shoulder again. "Now sit up and listen to me."

Quiet now, but with the tears still streaming down her face, Laura sat up and looked at Daddy. His blue eyes weren't angry any more.

"We're very lucky, Laura," he said gently. "You don't know how lucky. It was such a terrible accident. For a while we weren't even sure she would come out of it. But it's over now, and she's home. That's all that matters."

"I didn't know it was that bad," Laura sobbed.

"Shh, shh," Daddy whispered. "Maybe I should have told you, but what was the point of getting you all upset? You were upset enough as it was. Anyway, it's over now. Let's forget the whole thing. She's going to be all right, Laura. I promise you."

"But when?" Laura cried.

"Shh," Daddy whispered. "Soon. Maybe not tomorrow, but one day soon. She'll get up from that wheel chair and walk. You'll see. It won't be long. We'll even have her running one of these days."

There were tears in Daddy's eyes too as he continued. "But she's home now. That's the important thing. And we all have to do everything we can to help her get better and see that she's happy. Right, Laura?"

Laura nodded miserably.

"So no more crying in front of her. No more complaining or loud voices. Nothing unpleasant. Only cheerful faces and happy conversations. Right?"

Daddy took his handkerchief out of his pocket, wiped his eyes, and then Laura's. He waited while she washed her face at the kitchen sink and clumsily tried to pat her hair into place.

"Come on now, and don't forget what I said."

Together they walked back down the hall into the living room.

"Well, here's the missing link," Daddy said, laughing, with an arm around her shoulder. "We could have guessed why she was bawling like that. She didn't get a 100 on a test, poor thing."

"That Laura!" Aunt Minnie said, laughing heartily.

When she stopped laughing, the room suddenly grew very quiet. Laura stood motionless where she was, with Daddy's arm on her shoulder, until she felt his hand nudging her very gently. Slowly she walked toward Mama. What should she do? Should she kiss Mama? Could she kiss Mama? Would it hurt Mama if she put her arms around her neck? What was she supposed to do?

But Mama reached up and pulled her down against her and kissed her, and held her very tight. She had been waiting a long time to feel Mama's arms around her, but all she could think about was that Mama smelled different. She returned Mama's kiss and tightened her own arms around Mama's neck, but all the time she kept thinking about that smell. It reminded her of the time she had her tonsils out, and how much it hurt. Very embarrassed, and hoping that Mama couldn't know what she was thinking, she stood up suddenly and smiled helplessly.

"You're so tall, Laura," Mama murmured.

"Eats more than all the rest of us put together," Aunt Minnie chortled loudly, and she and Daddy began laughing. When they stopped, it grew very quiet again in the room.

"And your braces," Mama continued. "Do they hurt?"

Do they hurt? "Oh, Mama," Laura almost blurted out, "yes they hurt, and sometimes they feel like a ton of lead in my mouth, and most of the time I wish I didn't have to wear them." But there was Daddy, shaking his head carefully at her, so she said brightly, "Oh no, they feel fine. I — I don't mind them at all."

Then it grew quiet again, and Aunt Minnie said, "Laura, don't you have something for your mother?"

"Oh yes, I'll get it," Laura said gratefully. She hurried into her room, fished the fascinator out of the bottom drawer of her chest, and carried it back into the living room.

"I'm sorry, Mama," she said shyly. "I meant to wrap it, but you came back before I had a chance. I mean, I'm glad you did, but I just didn't have time."

Awkwardly, she laid the shawl in Mama's lap.

"Oh, Laura," Mama cried, "it's beautiful! Just beautiful. Did you do this all by yourself?"

"Aunt Minnie helped me," Laura admitted. She watched Mama holding the fascinator up and examining the stitches. Then Mama wrapped it around her shoulders and beamed up at Laura.

"Thank you darling, it's lovely."

And it was lovely. Laura knew it was. Such a delicate pink, and such lacy stitches! While she was making it, she used to think about how Mama would look wearing it. The picture in her mind had been of Mama stretched out on the couch, maybe in that pretty blue dress she used to wear, with her shiny brown hair and rosy cheeks. Right now, Mama was wearing a dress she had never seen before — a brown dress with dark flowers on it, and her hair was combed straight behind her ears and held back with two bobby pins. And her cheeks weren't rosy. Guiltily, Laura turned away and looked at Daddy. What should she do now?

Mama said, "Now I have something for you two. Harry, it's in the small suitcase on the bed."

Daddy went off to the bedroom and returned with two brown paper bags. "I made these in the hospital," Mama said, handing a package to each girl. Amy's bag contained a red crocheted beret with mittens to match. Laura's had a blue beret with blue mittens. Amy immediately pulled her hat over her curls and slipped her hands into the mittens.

"Ooh, they're pretty!" she glowed, and hurried into the bedroom to look at herself in the mirror.

"Go ahead, Laura, try it on," Aunt Minnie urged. "It's a good color for you."

Obediently, Laura trotted off to the bedroom, pulling on the beret as she went. Amy was standing in front of the mirror, smiling at her reflection. "I look so nice in this hat," she said admiringly. "Don't I, Laura?"

Amy's reflection looked gay and pink and sparkling. Above it, Laura saw her own face, puffy with tears, her hair unkempt, and the jaunty blue hat sitting uneasily on top of her head. "What a mess!" she groaned.

Amy's eyes in the mirror focused for a moment on Laura's reflection, and then, unwilling to waste any more time, returned to her own face.

"You look very nice too, Laura," she said politely, arching her neck and examining herself from a different angle.

"Where's my comb?" Laura said, ignoring the obvious flattery. She pulled off the hat, combed her hair, tucked her blouse in, and tried the hat on again. It certainly was a nice hat, and such a pretty blue, too. Mama had not forgotten that blue was her favorite color. The least she could do was show Mama how much she appreciated it, and stop looking so grim. She smiled at her reflection in the mirror. There now, that was better.

"Let's wear our hats to school tomorrow," Amy said, twisting around and looking over her shoulder at the mirror.

"Okay," Laura answered, examining a slightly wider smile. Then she remembered, and the smile spread quickly all over her face. "Amy!" she shouted. "I didn't tell you yet." She put her hand into her pocket, pulled out the star, and held it up for Amy to see. "Look, look, I'm a monitor."

"Gee!" said Amy respectfully.

Well now, this was something that would really make Mama happy. She flew back to the living room, laid the precious star in Mama's hand, and waited. Mama looked down at it and smiled. "What is it?" she asked.

"Oh, Mama," Laura said proudly. "I'm a monitor. I wear that. It happened today. Mrs. Foster told me after school. Tomorrow is my first day."

"What do you have to do?"

"I don't know exactly. Either I patrol the yards or I stand on the stairs when the kids go up, or I might be assigned to the traffic squad and see that nobody jaywalks."

"Do you have to stand in the street?" Mama asked, frowning.

Laura felt frightened suddenly. Naturally, after the terrible accident, Mama would be bound to worry about cars.

"Maybe I won't be on the traffic squad." Laura tried to sound cheerful. "But I'd be careful, Mama."

Mama turned the star over in her hand.

Her face was serious. "I don't think you should be on the traffic squad, Laura," she said.

"I'd really be careful if they put me there," Laura began desperately, but Daddy interrupted. He smiled at Laura, but said very firmly, "Just tell them you *can't* be on the traffic squad. Any other place is all right, but not the traffic squad. Right, Laura?"

"Oh sure," Laura said quickly, reaching down and taking back the star from Mama. She tried not to look worried. What would Stuart Johnson say when she told him she couldn't be on the traffic squad? Suppose that was the only place they wanted her to go. Would she have to give back her star?

"I'm sure it's a great honor," Mama said. "I'm really very proud of you, Laura."

Amy came into the room. She was wearing her good navy-blue coat, had changed into her patent-leather shoes, and was carrying her fancy patent-leather purse. She had stuck a rhinestone pin into the center of her beret and was carrying her mittens languidly in one hand, the way the actresses always do in the movies.

"Do you need anything at the store?" she asked hopefully.

Mama began laughing. "Same old Amy," she said. "She hasn't changed a bit, has she?"

"No," Aunt Minnie said a little sharply, but smiling too. "Any new thing, she has to run right out and show off to the whole world."

"I just want to help," Amy pouted.

"Sure you do, sweetheart, and you look lovely," Mama said soothingly.

"You certainly are handy, Hannah," Aunt Minnie said, eying Amy's hat. "It fits her perfectly." She glanced at Laura. "Pull your hat back a little, Laura. It's practically covering your eyes. I wish I could crochet as well as you do."

"You're not so bad yourself," Daddy said. "It isn't everybody who can make a pair of drapes like these."

Four pairs of worshipful eyes turned to the windows where the peacock-blue drapes hung, brilliant and brand-new. So many weeks of work had gone into getting them ready for Mama's return. Laura felt the joy begin to flow again inside her as she looked at them. Even if the day had not turned out as she had hoped, even if nobody in the room had been able to say all the splendid words Mama should hear on this her first day home, at least the new drapes hung there — an eloquent, loving gift of welcome from them all.

Laura turned her eyes to Mama's face. It

was serious, and her eyes blinked uncertainly as she turned and said slowly to Aunt Minnie, "How can I ever thank you for everything you've done. What would Harry ever have done if you..."

"Please, please," Aunt Minnie cried, shutting her eyes and waving her hand in dismissal of any thanks. "I've enjoyed every minute of it, and don't think you can get rid of me so easily. I'll be around for a long time to come."

"Minnie..." Mama said earnestly.

"Now that's all!" said Aunt Minnie firmly, reaching out and taking Mama's hand. "I'm glad you like the drapes. I ran right over there when I read about the fire in Drexler's, and there was this lady holding up a piece of the material and just looking at it. So right away I grabbed the other end of the material, called the man over, and said, 'I'll take it.' So she said, 'But I saw it first!' 'Well,' I said, 'but I'm buying it first.' "

Again all eyes in the room turned to the magnificent drapes. But Laura looked at them quickly, frowned, and turned to Mama. Mama's eyes were moving from the drapes, around the room. She shivered a little, drew the fascinator more tightly around her shoulders, and looked very tired.

"She never said she liked them," Laura

thought to herself. Why not? Her eyes followed in the path that Mama's had taken from the gleaming, brilliant drapes to the old sagging sofa, the faded green chair, and down to the worn rug. Daddy was always talking about how they were going to buy new furniture once the money came rolling in.

Aunt Minnie began telling Mama all the details about how much the material cost, how she really wasn't satisfied with the lining, and how Mrs. Murphy from upstairs turned absolutely green with envy when she saw them from outside.

"But it's all worth it," Aunt Minnie said, "as long as you enjoy them."

Mama smiled, looked again at the drapes, and nervously pulled at the pink fascinator around her shoulders. It was lovely, that fascinator, Laura thought sadly, even if Mama did look so pale and tired and worn. And then suddenly she knew why it was that Mama did not like the drapes. Because their beauty made everything else in the room look shabby and drab. They belonged with gleaming, new furniture in a room where everything shone with newness. Like the fascinator belonged — no, no, she didn't mean to think *that*.

"I think I'd like to rest for a little while," Mama said, smiling.

"That's a good idea," Aunt Minnie said heartily, jumping up from the couch. "I'll start supper." She frowned. "Although — you know we planned a real fancy welcome-home dinner for you tomorrow, but tonight I don't really have anything special in the house."

"Hot dogs," Amy yelled. "Let's have hot dogs. I'll go the delicatessen. Give me some money. I'll go right now."

"No you won't," snapped Aunt Minnie. "Your mother's not going to want to eat hot dogs."

"Sure I do," Mama said smiling, but looking very weary. "Let her get them. Please, Minnie."

Daddy wheeled the wheel chair over to their bedroom, helped Mama inside, and after a few minutes returned, closing the door softly behind him.

"Let's go outside," he whispered to the girls. "I want to talk to you."

They followed him out to the stoop. "From now on," Daddy said, "we're all going to have to watch our ways. No more fighting. No more shouting. No complaining. If anything bothers you, take it up with me outside. Whatever Mama tells you to do, do it. Don't forget!"

"Yes," Laura agreed, hanging her head. "And Daddy, I'll make sure I don't get put

on the traffic squad even if ... even if I have
to give up my badge."

"That's a good girl," Daddy said. "She'll
be fine. You'll see. And all of us have to do
everything we can to make her happy."

"Daddy," Amy said.

"What?"

"Can we have Pepsi-Cola tonight?"

"Sure," Daddy laughed. "It's a celebra-
tion, isn't it? Come on, I'll go with you.
Maybe we'll even buy a cake in the bakery."

"Chocolate!" yelled Amy.

"Chocolate," agreed Daddy.

Amy took Daddy's arm and began pulling
him. "Are you coming, Laura?" he asked.

"No. I think I'll go in and help Aunt Minnie."

"Fine." He and Amy began moving quickly
up the street.

Laura stood a few moments on the stoop,
watching them until they disappeared around
the corner. Then she looked up at their windows. The new drapes that had made Mrs.
Murphy turn green with envy only filled
Laura with helplessness. How could she ever
have liked them, and why in the world hadn't
she knit Mama a fascinator that was gray?

# Halloween

Three days before Halloween, Daddy brought Amy outside for a conference on the stoop.

"Now look," he said, "this has just got to stop! You're driving us all crazy with your costume for the party. Make up your mind, and stop bothering Mama."

"I'm not bothering Mama," Amy protested. "She says she'll help me, and she keeps giving me lots of good ideas."

"Now I want you to leave her alone. She needs a lot of rest, and with you running around, dragging everything out and chattering about what you're going to wear, she doesn't have a chance to relax."

"Well, what do you think I should be?" Amy asked.

"How do I know what you should be?" Daddy said irritably. "You're making a big fuss over nothing."

"What did you use to be for Halloween?" Amy said cozily, settling herself on the stone ledge and waiting for Daddy to tell one of his stories about what he did when he was a child.

But Daddy wasn't in a storytelling mood. He just snorted and said, "I didn't go around bothering my parents, I'll tell you that."

"Well, but what do you really think, Daddy? Should I be a witch or a nurse?"

"A witch," Daddy said immediately. "That's a very good thing to be for Halloween."

"But most girls dress up like witches," Amy said. "I want to be different."

"So be a nurse."

"Maybe I will be a nurse," Amy said happily, jumping off the ledge. "That's a good idea, Daddy."

"Fine. It's all settled." Daddy turned to go into the house.

"Daddy!"

"What?"

"What should I wear?"

Halloween night, Amy paused outside Helen's cellar door and giggled. A huge, life-sized cardboard skeleton hung on the door and grinned back at her. In the upper left-hand corner of the door a smaller black cardboard witch rode her broomstick, and down in both lower corners two wicked-looking black cardboard cats arched their backs.

She knocked on the door, and the bracelets on her arm jingled and jangled. She was dressed as a gypsy, and everybody in the household, even Daddy, had contributed something or other for the costume. She was wearing an old red skirt of Laura's that flared way out when she spun around. Tied around her head was a bright yellow scarf, also belonging to Laura. For a sash, Aunt Minnie had dug up a piece of purple, iridescent material that had once been part of a ball gown belonging to Aunt Harriet. Mama had found all sorts of old bits of jewelry, and Daddy had loaned her a pair of his suspenders to wear crisscrossed over her blouse. Amy had spent the last few days stringing necklaces of red, blue, and yellow beads. She wondered what the other girls looked like, and whether or not there would be a prize for the best costume. She adjusted the black mask across her eyes and watched as the door slowly creaked open.

All was darkness within. The light of the lamppost down the block shed only a little light inside, but Amy could hear unmistakable sounds of laughter. She blinked, and wondered if she should go on in. This was the first time she had ever visited Helen Prendergast, but she knew that Helen's father was the superintendent of the building and that the family lived in the basement behind the furnace room.

"Enter!" a deep, scary voice finally commanded.

Carefully, Amy took a step forward into the mysterious interior. Nothing happened. Even the laughter seemed to evaporate. Slowly she took another step, and with a loud bang, the door shut behind her. Quickly she turned and tried to see what or who stood in back of her, but all was completely dark and silent.

Giggling again, she peered in front of her, and could just make out a crack of light that seemed to be coming from way down the passageway in which she was standing. With both arms stretched out in front of her, Amy began walking toward the light.

"Whoooh!" moaned something behind her.

"Aaah!" screamed Amy, and began running. Plop. Something wet and clammy wrapped itself around her face and arrested her flight. Giggling very hard, Amy reached up and tried to untangle her face from the wet mass above her. "It's towels," she realized suddenly, "wet towels hanging from strings." The laughter which had returned seemed to be all around her as she carefully detached herself from the maze of towels and resumed her journey. Suddenly a faint light from one side of the hall began glowing, and out of the light three ghostly white-draped figures rushed at her.

Giggling and screaming, Amy was dragged forward into a large room filled with laughter. Here was the party. One of the white-draped figures pulled off the sheet, and there stood Helen, wearing a sarong made of striped turkish towels, with artificial flowers in her hair.

"Gee, that was fun." Amy laughed.

"You yelled louder than anybody else," Helen said approvingly.

There was another knock on the door, and Helen tossed the sheet over her head again and rushed off into the hall to greet her new guest.

Amy looked around happily. The big furnace room was lit only by the flickering fire in the coal burner, and one dim, naked bulb that hung from a wire in the middle of the ceiling. Black and orange streamers crisscrossed from one wall to another, and black and orange balloons floated above her head.

There were quite a few children in the room, most of them girls in her class, and all of them in costume.

"You look gorgeous, Amy," Rhoda Fleming said, and waited for Amy to say something about *her* costume. Rhoda was dressed like a bride, in a magnificent white-satin gown, with a filmy veil over her face and a bouquet of artificial flowers in her arms. It was just a little bit upsetting to see somebody in a costume maybe even prettier than your own, but then Amy wasn't sure there would be a prize for the best costume anyway. Now she hoped there wouldn't be.

"You look gorgeous too," she admitted generously.

"Look at *me*, Amy," Cynthia said, cavorting around her. Cynthia was dressed like a tramp in raggedy boy's clothes, an old cap on her head, a stick with a bandana tied to one end of it over her shoulder, and a huge pair of men's shoes on her feet.

The three ghostly figures dragged Frances Jackson, screaming and struggling, into the room, and bounded off as another knock was heard.

Amy laughed so hard, she had to sit down. Three more guests arrived, screaming and giggling, and then Helen's big sister, Patricia, filled a large basin with water, dropped a few apples into it, and they began bobbing for apples. When Amy's turn came, she knelt gingerly over the basin, her hands behind her back, and tried carefully to nibble a piece of the apple without getting her face too wet.

Splash! Somebody behind her had ducked her head into the water. Furiously, Amy jumped up, shaking the water from her face and hair, and feeling it dribble down her neck. She knew Cynthia had done it, even though Cynthia was now dancing merrily around the room, twirling her stick above her head.

"Look what you did," she grumbled. "I'm soaking wet."

"Who, me?" laughed Cynthia.

"I'll fix you," Amy said, drying herself with the towel Patricia handed her and starting off in pursuit of the elusive Cynthia. All around the room, and up and down the dark passageways the two girls ran. Golly, what a place! Full of all sorts of mysterious nooks and crannies. Amy hadn't realized what a wonderful house Helen lived in.

By the time the girls returned to the big furnace room, a game of Blind Man's Buff was in progress, and they were soon absorbed in darting here and there, shrieking and laughing away from "It."

When the noise had become absolute bedlam, Patricia said she thought this would be a good time to tell ghost stories. Everybody sat around the coal furnace, Helen turned off the overhead light, and it all felt just perfectly spooky. Helen told the first story. It was about a mummy who came back to life and terrorized a whole village. Everybody breathed a deep sigh of contentment when the mummy was finally pushed over a high precipice. Glancing sideways at Cynthia, who sat next to her, Amy said, "I know a good one," before anybody else did. So she was the next storyteller. She told the story of "The Golden Arm," and tried to work out the details exactly as Daddy did. This was his special story. He had told it to her once, and nearly scared the daylights out of her. Now it was her turn.

"Once upon a time," she began, keeping her voice low and mysterious, "there was a man who was very rich. He had everything his heart could desire except a wife. So he hunted high and low until he found the most beautiful woman in the whole world."

On and on Amy went, spinning out the details of the story. How a terrible accident had caused the wife to lose an arm. How the rich man had bought a golden arm for her. How she had died finally, and the rich man had lost all his money. How he had plundered the grave and taken the golden arm, which he hid under his pillow.

"And that night," Amy whispered, "there

came a great storm, and the wind howled outside his window." She paused, and listened with satisfaction to the complete, horrified silence around her. Cynthia sat motionless at her side. "I'll fix her now," Amy thought, and continued the story: "The man heard something coming up the stairs. Trembling with fear in his bed, he saw the door open, and there stood the ghost of his dead wife." Her voice dropped lower and lower as the questioning began.

" 'Where is your yellow hair?' the man asked.

" 'Gone in the grave,' the ghost answered.

" 'Where are your eyes of blue?'

" 'Gone in the grave.'

" 'Where are your lips of red?'

" 'Gone in the grave.' "

For the final question, Amy's voice was barely a whisper, so that all the listeners had to lean forward as she spoke.

" 'And where is your golden arm?'

" 'YOU'VE GOT IT!' " she shrieked as loud as she could, and grabbed Cynthia's arm.

Cynthia screamed. Everybody screamed except Annette de Luca, who said, "I've heard that story before."

A few more girls told stories, and just as Amy was beginning to wonder about refreshments, Helen said, "Now we'll have the scavenger hunt, and when everybody gets back, we'll eat."

This was the first time Amy had ever gone on a scavenger hunt, and she listened with delight as Helen explained what they had to do. First of all, each girl needed a partner. Helen held out a basket filled with colored ribbons, and everybody had to close her eyes, pick a ribbon out of the basket, and then find the other girl who had the same color ribbon. Amy closed her eyes and picked. Her ribbon was green. She looked hopefully at the ribbon in Cynthia's hand. Too bad. It was orange. Gladys Finkelstein had the other green ribbon, which wasn't too bad. Gladys was all right.

"Now," said Helen, after the pairing-off process had been completed. "Each set of girls will receive a piece of paper with five things written on it. The lists are all different. You have to go out into the street and hunt around until you find all the things written on the paper. The first two girls who get back here win a prize. And no fair buying anything. You can't spend any money. So get going."

"Let's hurry," Gladys urged. She and Amy rushed over to Helen, who stood by the door handing out the lists. The girls grabbed theirs, ran outside, and, standing under the lamppost, read the following:

A ball of string
1 lady's high-heeled brown shoe
2 drinking straws
1 black cat
2 paper clips

"We're going to win," Gladys said confidently. "Come on, let's go over to my house. I live across the street."

"But is that fair?" Amy asked. "I thought we had to find everything on the street."

"Sure it's fair," Gladys said, a note of experience in her voice. "Everybody does it, anyway. You just aren't allowed to spend any money. Come on!" She took Amy's arm and pulled her across the street. They hurried up the stairs of Gladys' house, opened her door, and hurried into the apartment.

"Ma, Ma," Gladys called, "can I take one of your brown shoes?"

Gladys' mother was listening to a program on the radio. "Why do you need one of my brown shoes?" she said mildly, still listening to the program.

"Just for a scavenger hunt. I'll bring it right back."

Gladys' mother laughed in response to something funny that was being said on the radio. "All right," she said good-naturedly, "take one of the old ones."

Gladys ran into her mother's room with Amy at her heels, fished a brown shoe out of the shoebag, and handed it to Amy.

"Here," she said, "hold this while I get the other things." She opened a desk in the bedroom and moved a few things around until she found two paper clips.

"Here, hold this!"

Off to the kitchen Gladys dashed with Amy right behind her. In the cabinet under the sink, Gladys produced half a ball of string.

"Here, hold this!"

She stood up and peered into another closet.

"Ma!" she called.

No answer.

"Ma!"

She hurried back to the living room with Amy puffing along behind her. "Ma," she said, "where are the straws?"

"Straws?" repeated her mother blankly, her eyes fastened on the radio.

"Please, Ma," Gladys cried, "we're in a hurry. We want to win. Where are the straws?"

"Oh!" her mother's face became thoughtful as she glanced at her daughter. "I think we're all out of straws."

"Shucks," said Gladys. "Come on, Amy. My aunt lives downstairs. We'll ask for straws. She's got a cat, too."

Both girls hurried off toward the door.

"Gladys!" her mother called.

"What?"

"Are you having a nice time?"

"Yes." Gladys opened the door, and began to rush out.

"Gladys!" her mother called again.

"What is it?" Gladys cried, bumping into Amy as she stuck her head back through the door.

"Don't be home late, Gladys. Tomorrow's school."

"I know, I know," Gladys answered, closing the door behind her.

She flew down a flight of stairs and hammered on one of the doors on the next landing. As soon as the door was opened, Gladys said, "Aunt Sadie, can I borrow your cat, and do you have some straws?"

"What do you want the cat for?" asked Aunt Sadie.

"For a scavenger hunt," Gladys explained. Her aunt looked confused. "Oh, it's all right,

Aunt Sadie. We're at a party across the street, and we just need the cat for a few minutes. I'll bring him right back."

"Well..." said Aunt Sadie.

"Oh, thanks, you're a doll." Gladys hurried into the kitchen and picked up the sleeping cat. "Now — do you have any straws?"

"But Gladys..." Amy began.

"No, I don't," said Aunt Sadie. "And bring him right back."

"Gladys!" said Amy.

"I will. Thanks a lot," Gladys cried, hurrying to the door.

"Gladys!" Amy cried.

"What is it?"

"It's the wrong color."

Gladys glanced down at the orange and white cat in her arms and back at Amy. "What do you mean?"

"It says a *black* cat on the list."

"Oh, that's right," Gladys cried in annoyance, and handed the cat to her aunt. "Now where can we get a black cat?"

"Mr. Rosen, the candy-store man, has a black cat," Amy said. Now it was her turn to display confidence. "He likes me a lot. We can borrow his cat, and he'll give us the straws too."

"Let's go!"

The girls flew off down the stairs, jumping two and three at a time. Outside in the street, other dark figures scurried here and there, but Amy and Gladys hardly noticed them as they ran the two blocks to the candy store. When they arrived, Mr. Rosen was standing in the open door of the store.

"Hello, Mr. Rosen," Amy began. "Could I borrow your cat?"

"Go 'way," yelled Mr. Rosen, "go 'way!"

"But Mr. Rosen," Amy said, smiling confidently, "it's me."

"I know it's you, and I'll tell your mother on you. All day, all night, crazy kids coming in, bothering me. Such a crazy holiday! I never heard of such a thing when I was a boy. Trick or treat! I'll trick or treat them!" Mr. Rosen shook his fist, retired into the store, and banged the door behind him.

"I thought you said he liked you?" demanded Gladys.

"He gets funny sometimes," Amy explained. She leaned on the gum-ball machine outside the store. "Now what? We don't have any straws in my house either."

Just then Mrs. Ludwig passed, heading for the store.

"Oh Mrs. Ludwig," Amy called to her neighbor on the second floor, rear. She moved away from the gum-ball machine.

"Yes?" Mrs. Ludwig paused and looked at Amy. "Amy Stern, you look so cute," she said, smiling.

"Please, Mrs. Ludwig, are you buying something in the candy store?"

"I'm going to have a malted," Mrs. Ludwig admitted.

"Well, could you just get two straws for us? We're at a party — it's a game. We need two straws, and Mr. Rosen won't let us come in."

Mrs. Ludwig nodded, and began walking into the store.

"And Mrs. Ludwig," Amy continued quickly, "please, Mrs. Ludwig, could you just hand the straws out to us before you drink your malted? We're in a terrible hurry."

"Sure, sure," Mrs. Ludwig said kindly. She moved off into the store, and after what seemed like ages, opened the door and handed out two straws. "Here, darling, have a good time," she said.

"Thank you, Mrs. Ludwig," Amy said gratefully, and then turned to Gladys. "Come on, let's go!"

"Go where?" Gladys said gloomily. "We still need a cat."

"Well, let's find one," Amy said. "There're always plenty of cats around."

They hurried down the street, but there were no cats anywhere. There were, however, plenty of boys. Two boys dressed like pirates chased them around the corner, swinging stockings filled with flour. Every time the stocking whammed against Amy, it left a white blob on her costume. One of the boys looked familiar. Amy stopped running and took a good look.

"Herbert Katz," she cried, "I'm gonna tell Mrs. Malucci on you tomorrow."

"Blah, blah, blah," said Herbert Katz, landing a perfect shot on Amy's red skirt.

"And I'll tell the principal too!" Amy shouted as Herbert Katz caught up with Gladys and left two white blobs on her witch costume.

"I hate boys. I really do," Gladys declared, trying to brush away the lingering white powder on her skirt.

"Look — over there —" Amy cried "— a cat!"

"Shh! Don't scare it," Gladys said.

Slowly they began moving toward the shadowy figure over near the schoolyard. The cat remained motionless, only its eyes blinking in the darkness.

"I think it's a black one," Amy whispered.

"Shh!"

When they were practically close enough

to put out an arm and touch it, the cat suddenly came to life, springing away from them and bounding down the street.

After him the two girls ran, across Prospect Avenue, down Boston Road, until the fugitive took temporary refuge under a parked car.

"Here, pussy, pussy, pussy," Amy crooned, kneeling on her hands and knees, and trying to peer underneath the car.

"Nice pussy, pussy, pussy," Gladys joined in a chorus.

"Do you have anything for him to eat?" Amy whispered.

"Are you kidding?" Gladys said crossly.

Amy put one arm carefully under the car. The cat scratched it.

"Ouch!" howled Amy, and the cat dashed out from beneath the car, hurtled up a wall, and disappeared.

"Now look what you did!" grumbled Gladys.

Amy licked the scratch. "I don't think he was a black one anyway," she said.

Wandering aimlessly now, the girls poked half-heartedly into various shadowy places. Two more boys came along, and chalked up their backs, but not another cat of any color could they find.

"Oh, what's the use? Let's go back," Gladys

said, sitting down on the fender of a parked car.

Amy studied the list again, and a splendid idea came to her. "You know," she said, "it says a *black* cat. It doesn't say a *live* black cat."

Gladys looked interested. "Yes?"

"We can bring back a cardboard cat. Come on, hurry! We'll take one of those cats off Helen's door. Oh, why didn't we think of it before!"

They began running again, but had to take a long detour when they spotted three stocking-whirling boys headed in their direction.

Breathless, they arrived finally at Helen's house. The two cardboard black cats were still arching their backs wickedly on the door. Gladys pulled one off. "Maybe we'll still win," she said. "Maybe nobody else is back yet." They knocked at the door. Nobody answered. They knocked again, louder. Helen opened the door. "We thought you went home," she said.

"Did everybody come back already?" Amy asked as they followed Helen down the hall.

Everybody had come back long ago, and they were now seated around a big table, eating hot dogs and cupcakes and drinking orange soda. Annette de Luca and Rhoda Fleming had won the scavenger hunt.

"But they didn't have to look for a black cat," Gladys whispered sourly in Amy's ear. "All they had to find was a dead fish, two empty milk bottles, one license plate, three hard-boiled eggs, and one hat with a feather in it. That's easy."

"Yeah," Amy agreed. But as she took her first greedy bite into her first succulent hot dog and eyed contentedly the large stack of orange and black frosted cupcakes that still remained, all feelings of injustice quickly evaporated. So what if they didn't win a prize, she thought. There were other things in life besides prizes.

# The Monitor

Laura stood on the second landing of the up staircase where she had been posted as monitor, and thought about her problems. There were two of them: Veronica Ganz and Amy. Concerning her first problem, Veronica Ganz, she still had not made up her mind. Veronica was the toughest, meanest kid in school. Not a day passed without some child or other displaying on his or her body unmistakable signs of Veronica's wrath. She talked in a loud voice as she came up the stairs, laughed, and yesterday had even stuck out her tongue at Laura as her line passed.

Laura had been warned about Veronica by the other monitors. Even Stuart Johnson, the captain, had advised her just to ignore Veronica. Nobody had ever reported her. "No point in dying young," said Stuart.

Well, Laura didn't know about that. Justice was justice, and if it was wrong for one person to talk on line, then it was wrong for everybody else. But Veronica was easily a head taller than she was, had tight, hard muscles on her arms and legs, and a look in her frosty blue eyes that made Laura uncomfortable. Today, as her line passed in front of Laura, Veronica was singing in a loud, stupid voice:

I'll be down to get you in a taxi, honey,
Better be ready 'bout half-past eight,
Oh, honey, don't be late ...

shaking her hips, and making everybody around her giggle. Laura clenched her teeth and decided she was just going to have to do something about Veronica. But not today. Today was Amy's day. Veronica passed, and Laura could hear the singing continuing up to the next landing. Maybe tomorrow.

She fingered the pad of pink report slips in her hand and prayed that she wouldn't have to do it. But she had given Amy her last warning this morning, before she left for school. "I mean it," she told Amy. "This time I really mean it." And Amy had snickered and said, "Oh, don't be such a crab."

For over a week now, since Laura first took up her assignment on the second landing of the staircase, Amy had whispered and giggled as her line passed, just as if she knew she could get away with it because her sister was the monitor there. Showing off, that's what she was doing. Showing off and having a bad influence on the children around her. Laura set her mouth in a firm, straight line over her teeth and thought about the bold, sly looks in the eyes of Amy's classmates as they too whispered and giggled. Naturally they knew she could hardly pull them out of line and report them when her own sister was behaving worse than anybody else.

Not that Laura enjoyed pulling children out of line and reporting them. She knew some of the monitors strutted around like chiefs of police, puffed up with a sense of their own power. But for Laura, being a monitor wasn't scaring people but helping them, really. That's why the squad was called "Service Squad." If somebody fell, for instance, the monitor held up the line and helped the child up. If books were dropped, again the monitor came to the rescue. If somebody felt sick, the monitor arranged for the person to leave the line. If somebody mistakenly and dangerously started walking down the staircase while everybody else was coming up, the monitor redirected the wanderer to the down staircase.

Laura had reported only one girl since assuming her post. And that girl had pushed the child behind her, nearly causing the entire line to fall backward. It could have been very serious, but fortunately no one had been hurt. However, Laura felt the culprit deserved punishment. In general, though, she would try warning any evildoer, and usually the crime was not repeated. She tried, as she stood there on the landing watching the lines pass, to assume a firm but kind expression, so that if anybody really needed some kind of help or information, he wouldn't be scared off. Some of the monitors, Laura remembered from her premonitorial days, looked so fierce a child was almost afraid to pass before them.

Laura loved being a monitor. If it were not for Veronica Ganz and Amy, her satisfaction would be 100 per cent. If, for instance, both of them had classrooms on the other side of the building, and used the other up staircase, what a perfect world it would be. But Laura figured, although no one had told her so, that the reason she was assigned to this particular staircase was that she was one of the newest members of the squad. Which was not unreasonable after all. In fairy tales, you had to fight the dragon before you won the kingdom, and here you had to contend with Veronica Ganz and Amy before you could be assigned to a loftier position.

But what a joy it was to be so important to so many people! Bookworm that she was, Laura had never been too interested in the big world that lay outside her home and her books. She was still a bookworm, but now, for a half an hour in the morning and a half an hour in the afternoon (on the corresponding down staircase), she contributed toward making that world a better place. That's the way it seemed to her. The significance of her work was both dazzling and unsettling.

"Don't take it all so seriously," Mama urged, which was a strange thing for Mama to say, but then Mama seemed so different these days. Laura licked her braces. My, it was a comfort having braces to lick.

She put all thoughts of Mama away now, and focused her mind on Amy. The lines that moved all the way to the fourth floor had come and gone, and now the third-floor classes, which included Amy's class, began to appear. First Mrs. Daugherty's class — here they came now — a little fluttery maybe, but orderly. She shook her head at one girl who was humming. The humming stopped. Good! Now Mrs. Malucci's class, Amy's class. "Please, please," she thought, "let it be all right. Let her behave. I can't do it. My own sister!"

Mrs. Malucci's class was restless even before Amy appeared. Whispering, furtive giggling, those familiar sly glances at her. Laura shook her head and frowned. One of the girls stumbled and dropped her books. A wave of laughter swept through her companions. Laura stopped the line, waited until the child had collected her belongings, and said firmly, "Now no more noise, or I'll report all of you." It helped — a little. The line began moving again, and there, halfway up the staircase, in plain view now, came Amy. Laura's face darkened, and she cast a serious "I mean business" look at her sister. She could see the danger signs on Amy's face — her eyes sparkling, her cheeks pink, her lips pressed tightly together as if some explosive force lay behind them.

"Please, please," Laura prayed, "not today anyway. Tomorrow. Let it be tomorrow."

But then it happened. Amy's gay laughter came floating up the stairs. "I can't stand it," Laura heard her say out loud. "It's so funny." And all the children around her laughed too, and nudged each other and looked fearlessly at Laura.

"It's not their fault," she thought sadly, "and I've got to do it."

"Step out!" she ordered, as her sister climbed the last step to the landing.

Amy made a face and kept walking. More laughter from the children around her.

"I said, step out of line," Laura repeated, stopping the line.

Amy's face was merry. "All right, Sis, I'll

be good now," she said. Ordinarily, Amy never called her "Sis," and although Laura felt the appeal that lay behind the word, it was not going to save Amy now. It was too late.

She took Amy's arm and pulled her out of line. The laughter stopped. "All right," Laura ordered the other children, "go ahead now!"

"Laura . . ." Amy began.

"Be quiet!" Laura said. "I'll speak to you after the lines go up."

When the last child had disappeared from the staircase, Laura turned and faced her sister. Amy's face was angry and pale. "Now what am I going to tell Mrs. Malucci?" she demanded. "I'll have to say I was late."

Laura began writing on her pad.

NAME: Amy Stern
CLASS: 5B¹
ROOM: 312
BEHAVIOR: Talking, laughing, and disturbing the line on the up staircase

"You won't have to tell Mrs. Malucci anything," she said tersely. "I'll do all the talking."

"Laura, are you crazy or something?" Amy cried.

"Let's go," Laura answered. "I warned

you over and over again, and you didn't listen."

"But, Laura," Amy said in amazement, "you're my sister!"

"I wish I wasn't," Laura said bleakly. She took Amy's arm and started walking her up the stairs. Angrily, Amy pulled her arm away and hurried up by herself. Outside Room 312, Amy paused, bit her lip, and said urgently, "You know how mean she is. She hates me anyway. She'll really punish me."

Laura put her arm out to open the door.

"Laura," Amy spoke with a sob in her voice. "How can you be like this? I'd never do this to you."

But Laura, feeling a sob rising in her own throat, opened the door as quickly as she could and entered first.

Mrs. Malucci, passing out yellow papers, turned and faced them, large and unsmiling.

Laura handed her the pink slip and waited in case the teacher had any questions. She realized that Amy was standing in the doorway, because she could see the eyes of every child in the class focused in that direction. She felt empty — neither good nor bad — just empty.

Mrs. Malucci read slowly, nodded, and said to Laura, "Thank you. I'll see that it doesn't happen again." Then her eyes followed the children's eyes to the figure in the doorway. "Come over here!" she rumbled.

Laura turned and saw Amy's face. Two pink spots on her cheeks, her lips trembling, her eyes already overflowing with tears as she approached the teacher. Laura fled.

This was the longest day in Laura's life. Amy's scared, tearful face followed her everywhere. She knew she had done the right thing, the fair thing, and that, if necessary, she would do it again. But she ached in every part of her body. During lunch Laura forced herself not to seek Amy out. How could she talk to her in front of all the others? How could she explain the principles involved in all this with hundreds of kids around? She would talk to her after school at home. She would make her understand.

But what would Mrs. Malucci do to Amy? Her hatred for Mrs. Malucci grew savage. Any other teacher would just reprimand a child who had been reported, or perhaps lower the conduct mark on her report card. But that big, mean bully! What would she do to Amy? Little Amy. A nice kid really, a good kid too. The way she had spoken to Amy in that terrible voice — "Come over here!" What kind of a way was that to talk to a nice little kid like Amy? What a monster that teacher was!

Laura licked her braces without comfort. Maybe Mrs. Malucci would have Amy do a punishment paper, something like "I will not talk on the staircase" one hundred times for homework. "I'll help her with it," Laura thought. "I can even do the whole thing for her." And then, there was that blue beaded purse she had that Amy admired so much. Maybe she ought to give it to Amy to keep. After all, how much did she use it anyway?

Amy avoided her eyes on the down staircase at three o'clock. Mrs. Malucci's class had never behaved better. Straight lines, no whispering, no giggling. It was a triumph for Laura, but an empty one, as her beseeching eyes followed her sister's averted face.

She hurried home after her duties had been completed, rehearsing all the eloquent reasons she would present to Amy. Also, she had fifty cents in her bank at the moment — enough to treat Amy to a chocolate soda, and a pretzel stick too. And she'd definitely give her the beaded purse, and definitely do the punishment paper too. Was there anything else she could do?

Amy's sobs could be heard very distinctly outside the door. Laura took a deep breath, opened the door, and followed the sobs into the living room. Amy was a miserable little bundle in one corner of the couch, and

Mama, in the wheel chair, was leaning over her.

Amy looked up as Laura entered the room, and her sobs grew into howls. Mama also looked up, and before Laura could say anything, she said, kind of bewildered, "Laura, is all this true?"

"But Mama . . ." Laura began.

"I can hardly believe it," Mama interrupted. "Did you actually report Amy to her teacher? *Report your own sister?*"

There it was again — that "your own sister" business, She never, in a million years, thought Mama would say that.

"But Mama," Laura explained, "she was talking and laughing on line. She's been doing it for days. I warned her over and over again. She made all the kids in her class behave badly. It was dangerous, too. Somebody could have fallen and broken a leg or something."

"She's your sister, Laura," Mama said, shaking her head.

"But what's that got to do with it?" Laura replied earnestly. "What kind of a monitor would I be if I reported other people and let her get away with it? Don't you see, Mama? It just wouldn't be fair."

"No," Mama insisted. "You should have come to me. I would have spoken to her."

Laura remained silent. How could she tell Mama that she hadn't wanted to upset her or burden her with any disagreeable problem?

"You know," Mama said slowly, "Amy has her faults, but I don't think she would ever do a thing like this to you. The most important thing for you to remember is that your own family comes first."

Laura moved uneasily from one foot to the other.

"That's what a family is for!" Mama continued. "Nothing is more important than that."

Laura cleared her throat. "Mama," she said unhappily, "I don't really believe that."

Mama looked worried. "I don't know," she said. "You've changed since you became a monitor. You used to look after Amy in the old days — protect her, and see that nobody hurt her. That's the way a big sister should be."

Laura walked out of the room and kept away from everyone for the rest of the afternoon. It was astonishing, but for the first time in her life she knew that Mama was wrong. And that there *were* some things more important than your own family. However, that night in bed she addressed Amy's shoulder, since Amy's face was turned stubbornly to the wall. She presented all the eloquent arguments she had rehearsed on the way home from school, plus a few others, offered the beaded purse, and suggested a trip to the candy store on the next day. Amy refused to speak. The following morning, though, she loftily accepted the purse and agreed to meet Laura in the candy store after school. But in regard to Laura's eloquent statement of principle, Amy could only say that it was "full of baloney."

# A Code of Honor

"So then what did you say?" Daddy asked.

It was the following night, after supper, and Laura and Daddy were standing outside on the stoop, holding another conference.

"Well I said, 'Suppose she killed somebody?'"

"And what did Mama say?"

"She said, 'Whatever she did, she's still your sister. I'm surprised at you, Laura.'"

Laura's face was full of pain. "She just didn't understand. I kept trying to explain to her all afternoon about the principles involved and why I just had to report Amy, but she just didn't understand."

Daddy shook his head and grinned. "Amy really had it coming to her, I guess, but you were wrong to report her because you should have realized that Mama would be upset."

Laura nodded. Of course Daddy was right about not upsetting Mama, but aside from that, she hadn't really expected Daddy to understand anyway. Everything always seemed to be a big joke to him. Like that pin he was wearing on his lapel right now. It had a star on it, which meant that he was in favor of the Democratic party winning the election next week. But Laura knew that on the underside of his lapel was another pin, with an eagle on it, which meant that he was in favor of the Republican party. Daddy's present job was selling insurance, and whenever he visited a prospective client whose political sentiments were in favor of the Democratic party, he would wear the button with the Democratic star on the top of his lapel. However, if he visited a client who was voting for the Republican party, he would show the one with the Republican eagle.

"When in Rome, do as the Romans do," he explained.

This was an incredible way of looking at things, to Laura. Not only incredible, but shocking as well. She knew Mama felt the same way she did. Or at least in the old days Mama would have felt the same way. Because always, in matters involving truth and justice, the lines had been sharply drawn in the Stern family: Mama and Laura on one side, Daddy and Amy on the other. But Laura was no longer sure of how Mama felt, and the question in her mind grew larger and larger as each day passed.

"I'll talk to Amy," Daddy said, "and make sure she behaves herself." He sighed. "And even if she doesn't behave herself, don't report her again. Don't do anything that would upset Mama. Right, Laura?"

"Right, Daddy," Laura agreed with an effort.

But Daddy must have really impressed Amy. He spoke to her later that evening, also outside on the stoop. And the next day in school, when she walked up the stairs she made sure to keep her eyes off Laura, lest she be tempted again. And, gratefully, Laura made sure to keep her own eyes focused somewhere off in the distance when her sister appeared.

For two whole days Laura had been too upset to do anything about Veronica Ganz. But now on the third day, with the problem of Amy behind her, the sap of righteousness began flowing again in Laura's veins. As she watched Veronica's performance on the staircase that morning, she knew that the day of reckoning had arrived.

Veronica, coming up the stairs, had grabbed the books from the girl behind her and was balancing them on her head and trying to walk up the stairs at the same time. Naturally she failed. The books fell down the staircase, and the lines became a giggling, arguing mass of confusion.

Grimly Laura strode down the stairs.

"Come on, Veronica, please give me back my books," whined the girl behind her.

Veronica was still balancing one or two on her head.

"Give her back her books!" Laura ordered.

"Why, sure," Veronica leered. She tossed the books over the heads of the children in front of her and stood grinning at Laura.

"Pick up your books," Laura said to the other girl, "and you," she took a deep, angry breath and looked right up at Veronica, "you step out of line!"

For one moment Veronica looked baffled. "Step out of line," she repeated, "*me* — step out of line?"

"Yes, *you!*" Laura held up the line until all the books had been restored to their owner, and then she returned to the landing, looked back down at Veronica, and motioned her to come.

"Why, I'd love to, honeybunch," Veronica cooed. "I'd go anywhere with you."

Grinning a wide, evil grin, Veronica Ganz leaped up the stairs and stood right up close to Laura. "Why, I'll even be glad to help," she said.

Motioning with her arms, as if she were a traffic policeman, Veronica started shouting orders. "Right ... Left ... Stop ... Go!" She tried to get some of the children in her class to go through the doorway that led to the second floor, even though the fourth floor was their destination.

"Now stop it!" Laura ordered sharply. "And go stand over there!" She pointed to the corner of the landing where offenders were supposed to huddle quietly until the lines had gone up and the monitor could attend to them. She was so angry and outraged at Veronica's behavior, she almost forgot to be afraid. Almost.

Obediently, Veronica moved into the corner and began dancing a Lindy Hop. The lines rocked with laughter. By the time Amy's class came climbing up the stairs, Veronica was once more standing next to Laura, giving traffic signals. Amy's eyes, in wonder this time, focused first on Veronica and then on Laura.

"Get back in that corner!" she heard Laura say wearily. Amy's mouth dropped open. She fixed a long, pleading look on her sister's face. "Don't do it," the look said. "In spite of everything, you're still my sister. Don't do it!"

But, impatiently, Laura motioned Amy on. Somehow or other, the lines actually made it up the stairs, and Laura found herself finally alone on the staircase with Veronica Ganz.

"What's your name, kid?" said Veronica, her blue eyes narrowing.

"Act like you don't know who she is," Laura told herself nervously, wondering if Veronica might push her down the stairs. She lifted the pink pad, poised her pencil over it, and said tonelessly, "Name?"

"Florence Nightingale," said Veronica Ganz.

Laura wrote "Veronica Ganz" on the slip.

"Class?" she tried next.

"1B¹," said Veronica in a little baby voice.

"8B⁴," wrote Laura.

She didn't bother asking the room number. She knew it was 406. Under BEHAVIOR, she hesitated and then wrote, "Is always bad and noisy on the stairs."

Somehow the words didn't seem to do justice to Veronica Ganz's behavior, but this was no time to worry about adjectives. Standing all alone with Veronica Ganz on the staircase, a helpless, ragged sense of terror began rising inside of Laura. She hoped her voice wouldn't tremble as she prepared to speak.

"You can go now. I'll be up later," she said.

But Veronica remained where she was. Her face didn't look at all mean or menacing. She even began smiling as she said almost gently to Laura, "You know what'll happen to you if you bring that slip up?"

"Go ahead," said Laura. She decided she would get away from that landing, go through the doorway to the second floor, and up the other staircase to Veronica's room. She had to get away — fast.

But as she opened the door and tried to move through it, Veronica's hand dropped to her shoulder and spun her around again. The fingers on her shoulder were like claws, but Veronica's face was still pleasant.

"You know who I am?" she asked.

"I know who you are," Laura answered, her knees shaking, "and let go of me."

"I'm Veronica Ganz," said Veronica. Her fingers pressed hard on Laura's shoulder, very hard. There was no escaping from that grip, and Laura wondered if she should scream. "And if you bring that slip up to my room," Veronica continued, "you'll never forget me as long as you live." She smiled tenderly at Laura, and then shoved her so hard through the door to the second floor that Laura ended up on the ground, the pink pad and pencil still spinning around in the air.

Through the open door Laura could hear Veronica whistling and the sound of her steps on the stairs.

She picked up the pad and pencil, brushed herself off, and wondered what to do next. Should she wait until tomorrow to deliver the slip? Should she seek out Stuart Johnson and ask his advice? Should she forget the whole thing? Really, that was the most attractive idea of all. Forget the whole thing, and just try to look amused from now on whenever Veronica Ganz passed her on the stairs. Just laugh the whole thing off.

She walked slowly across the second floor to the other up staircase and began climbing.

"After all," she told herself, "everybody knows the kind of girl Veronica Ganz is. Her teacher knows, the principal knows, the whole school knows. What difference is it going to make whether or not I report her? She probably always gets a D in conduct as it is. You can't get anything worse than that, can you?"

She stood outside Room 406 and thought, "Why do I have to be the one?" But there it was: she was the one. Opening the door, Laura moved swiftly into the classroom and up to the teacher's desk. She looked neither to the right nor to the left, but laid the pink slip in the teacher's hand, waited until she said "Thank you," turned swiftly, and left.

Amy sought her out in the lunchroom at noon. "Laura," she said, "I think you're crazy."

Laura continued chewing her sandwich gloomily. Now that her great act of heroism lay quietly behind her, only a continuing sense of panic remained.

"Are you going to tell your teacher?" Amy demanded.

Laura shrugged. "What's the use?"

"Veronica'll murder you," Amy said. "Did you see what she did to Jenny Wurster the other day? And that was for nothing. She said Jenny was laughing at her, but Jenny was only laughing at a joke Renee Holtzman was telling."

Laura winced. She knew with certainty that Veronica Ganz would be waiting for her after school that day, and she also knew with equal certainty that nothing could save her.

"Tell your teacher," Amy urged. "Maybe a grownup could take you home."

"So she'll get me some other time and it'll be worse then. May as well get it over with," Laura said honestly. "I haven't got a chance."

"Look, Laura," Amy said practically, "how about leaving by the Franklin Avenue door? She'll be waiting for you around the other side of the school. You could scoot up Franklin Avenue and go home the long way. Maybe if you did that for a few days she'd forget about it. She's always so busy beating up other kids, maybe she'd forget about you.

Maybe she'd even think she'd beaten you up after a couple of days beating up other kids."

"I doubt it," Laura said, but a faint — very faint — glimmer of hope began shining. "I could try," she said finally. "What have I got to lose?"

"Okay," Amy said, "and I'll wait for you and go home with you."

"No you won't."

"Yes I will!" Amy insisted. "I could go out the door first and see if she's waiting there."

"But maybe she'll hurt you too," Laura said weakly.

"Somebody's got to look after you," Amy said, sounding as if she was forgetting that she was the kid sister.

But Laura allowed the liberty to pass. It was good to think that Amy wasn't such a coward after all, and comforting to know that Amy would be there at three fifteen, willing to risk a bloody nose for her sake. Many a bloody nose had Laura risked for Amy's sake in the past, but nothing approaching the magnitude of the bloody nose somebody like Veronica Ganz could bestow. And besides, you'd think that after the way Laura had reported Amy, she just might feel Laura had it coming to her.

"You're a good kid," Laura said huskily.

"You're a dope," said Amy.

As Veronica Ganz passed Laura on the staircase at three o'clock that afternoon, she sang out sweetly, "See you later, honey-bunch." Laura tried looking unconcerned, but her heart pounded so loud she felt as if the whole school was shaking.

Amy was waiting for her inside the Franklin Avenue exit.

"All set?" she whispered.

"Yes."

"Stay back!"

"Okay."

Amy opened the door a crack and peeped out. She opened the door wider and stuck her whole head through, turning it quickly from side to side. Then she stepped outside and looked around casually, as if somebody was supposed to meet her there. Then she walked down the stairs to the sidewalk and looked intently up and down the block.

"Come on," she called to Laura, who was still hidden behind the crack in the door. Laura hurried down the steps, trying not to look at anything but Amy. They rushed to the corner and waited for the light to change. Suddenly there were quick footsteps behind them and a familiar hand on Laura's shoulder. "Looking for me, honeybunch?"

The light must have changed then, because even with that fearful hand on her shoulder and the ground trembling beneath her feet, Laura could see Amy dashing across the street and flying off in the distance. "Going for help," Laura thought. But their house was five blocks away. So figuring five blocks there and five blocks back — ten blocks — Laura abandoned hope.

"Should I catch her, Veronica?" came another voice. It was Mary Rose, Veronica's younger sister, who was in Amy's class, and a skinny, whiny shadow of her illustrious older sister.

"Don't bother," came Veronica's voice lazily. "It's not going to take long."

She dragged Laura away from the street corner and arranged her conveniently against the wall of an apartment house, then stuck her own face right up close to Laura's. Laura tried struggling. She tried kicking. She tried to loosen those hands pinning her against the wall. Veronica laughed, and waited until the throes subsided.

"You know what I'm going to do to you?" she asked gently. "I'm going to give you two black eyes."

"Yeah," said Mary Rose.

"And I'm going to give you a bloody nose."

"Yeah," said Mary Rose.

"And I'm going to —" Veronica began describing all the colorful changes that she was going to make in Laura's face.

"Yeah," said Mary Rose.

Veronica pressed her fingers harder and harder into Laura's shoulders as the gruesome list expanded.

"And she even reported her own sister." That was Mary Rose.

"Her own sister?" repeated Veronica.

There it was again. Was there no corner of the world where Laura could escape from *that?* "Oh, shut up!" she shouted.

Veronica loosened her hold on Laura's shoulder just a little and said curiously, "Your own sister? Why'd you do that for?"

"Mind your own business!" Laura snapped. "And leave my sister out of it."

"Come on, why'd you do that for?" Veronica was shaking her now.

"Because," Laura shouted, "she was talking and laughing on line. That's why."

"So why did you report her?" Veronica insisted.

And Laura told her why. She told her about the oath monitors took before they assumed their duties, to be fair and honest and just to all. She told her about the principles involved in Amy's case. About her feeling that what was bad for one person to do was likewise bad if someone else did it. About Mama. About how she liked being a monitor. About her code of honor.

And as she talked, Veronica Ganz slowly removed her hands from Laura's shoulder and stood listening.

Mary Rose kept interrupting, shouting, "Come on, Veronica, hit her, hit her!"

But Veronica sat down on a step and said to Laura, "What would you do if she murdered somebody?"

And Laura felt like kissing her. She could have run away then. Maybe she could have made it all the way home without being caught, but she sat down next to Veronica Ganz and began talking very earnestly to her. She explained that this thought was troubling her too, and frankly she just didn't know what she'd do, but honor was honor and trust was trust, and as long as she was a monitor she had to report everybody — but everybody who did something bad, regardless of who that person was. Didn't Veronica think that was the right thing to do?

"Yes," Veronica finally said. She did think it was the right thing. But she didn't think she could rat on her own sister, even if it was the right thing to do.

Mary Rose, a forlorn, restless figure above them, whined, "Aren't you going to hit her, Veronica?"

"You know," Veronica said, looking hard at Laura, "this is the first time anybody ever reported me."

"I know," Laura said. "They're all scared of you."

"Are you scared of me?" Veronica demanded.

Laura wished she didn't have to say it. They'd been having such a nice talk. Would it end with Veronica beating her up after all?

"Yes," Laura admitted. "I'm scared of you."

Veronica laughed. "Have you got any money?" she asked, getting up and pulling Laura up.

"I've got a dime," Laura said, feeling it in her coat pocket.

"Let's get a candy bar," Veronica said, holding out her hand.

Laura put the dime into her hand. Just then Mary Rose yelled, "Hey, look! Somebody's coming."

Sure enough, up the street came Aunt Minnie, a scrubbing brush in her hand. Behind her galloped Amy.

"That your mother?" Veronica said, motioning toward the advancing party.

"No — my aunt."

Aunt Minnie's speed was astonishing. It was also humiliating to Laura, but Veronica laughed as she turned and began walking languorously toward the curb.

"Looks like I'll have to eat the candy bar all by myself," she said.

And as Aunt Minnie hurried up to Laura, Veronica shouted from halfway across the street, "Hey, you!"

"Yes?" said Laura.

"If my sister gives you any trouble, you can report her. It's all right with me."

Mama was pale and frightened when they arrived home. She held Laura tight in her arms and looked carefully at her face.

"It's all right, Mama," Laura laughed. "She didn't hurt me. She's really a very intelligent girl. I explained how a monitor has to report everybody, and she — "

"Laura," Mama said in a high voice, "I want you to give up being a monitor."

"But Mama," Laura cried, "she didn't hurt me. She understood! Isn't that wonderful? Nothing else bad can happen to me now."

"Tomorrow," Mama insisted, "I want you to tell your teacher that you can't be a monitor any more."

"Please, Mama," Laura pleaded, "after

this, it'll be all right. It really will. Listen to me, Mama."

But Mama turned away, and Laura knew there could be no further appeal. She stood there forcing back the tears and all the protests that were crowding inside of her. She had promised Daddy that she would do whatever Mama asked, and she would keep her promise. Quickly she turned and hurried out of the room. A miracle had taken place that afternoon, but Mama had not understood, because Mama had changed inside as well as out. Laura knew that now for sure. To only one person had she been a hero, and that person was Veronica Ganz.

# Pancakes

Amy looked out of the window and made a face. Wouldn't you just know it! All week long, while she was sitting in school, the sun shone; but come Saturday, it had to rain. She tiptoed back into the bedroom and started to dress. Laura lay fast asleep in bed, a serious frown on her face. Funny how smart Laura looked even when she was sleeping. Maybe today Laura would be able to help her with that stupid "My Best Friend" composition. She still hadn't handed it in, and Mrs. Malucci seemed to have forgotten all about it. Just the same, it lay nagging and teasing at the back of Amy's mind. One of these days, she knew for sure, Mrs. Malucci would remember. Like an elephant, Mrs. Malucci never forgot.

But lately Laura seemed busy all the time. She was never home any more the way she used to be. Busy, busy, busy! Every afternoon she went off someplace, and didn't get back until suppertime. In the evenings she did her homework, and no one could get a word out of her. It was very annoying, that's what it was. How was she ever going to get that composition written if Laura didn't give her some ideas?

She stared at Laura's sleeping face with deep concentration, willing her to wake up. Laura stirred. Amy stared harder, gritting her teeth and furrowing her forehead. Laura turned over on her side, the side facing the wall. Well, she'd just have to wait until Laura woke up — probably not until eight or nine o'clock at least.

Amy finished dressing, walked back into the living room, and looked at the clock on the radio cabinet. Six twenty-five. She stole a hopeful look into her parents' bedroom, but no one was stirring there either.

Might as well read then. She picked up her library book from the bookcase and felt a contented glow of anticipation. This was the *Olive Fairy Book* by Andrew Lang, the only one of the colored fairy books that she had not read. For months she had pursued this book in vain at the library. All the others, which she'd already read, always seemed to be in: the orange, the yellow, the red, the blue, the silver, the gold. Finally, a few weeks ago, she became so desperate that she even asked Miss Roper, the librarian, if it might have been misplaced on another shelf. Miss Roper had looked, said "No," and shown her a number of other fairy-tale books. Miss Roper was being so pleasant that Amy didn't have the heart to tell her she'd already read all those others, or just didn't care for the looks of them. So she smiled, thanked Miss Roper, and put all the books back on the shelf when she wasn't looking. Then Amy had to hang around the library for at least an hour or so until Miss Roper left the desk, so she could check her books out without Miss Roper seeing that she wasn't taking any of the ones she had recommended. She didn't want Miss Roper to feel unhappy.

But then yesterday at the library, Miss Roper had come up to her as she was looking sadly through the fairy-tale section and had handed her the *Olive Fairy Book*.

"I've been saving this for you," she said.

Amy was so grateful that she had even taken out a book called *Beautiful Joe* that Miss Roper recommended. Ordinarily, she didn't care for dog stories, but she certainly would read this one, and make herself enjoy it too, for Miss Roper's sake.

She sat herself down in the old green club chair by the window and held the *Olive Fairy Book* closed in her lap for a few moments. She always did this with any new book, held it closed until she couldn't stand the suspense any longer. This one she kept closed maybe a little longer than usual, since she had been hungering for it for so long. She even pretended to be thinking of other things, and let her eyes wander around the room. They lighted on the wheel chair on the other side of the window. Amy stood up, looked again into her bedroom. Laura lay motionless. She tiptoed over to her parents' bedroom. Everybody sleeping there too. So very slowly and very quietly, she made her way back to the wheel chair. She ran her hand up and down the smooth arm rest, took one more cautious look around, and sat down in it. How she loved it! Every opportunity she had, when nobody was around, she sat in it. She'd miss it when they took it away. Not that she wanted Mama to be sitting in it much longer, she thought hurriedly, but it would be nice if they could just keep it around as a piece of furniture. It certainly was as beautiful as any other chair they had.

She leaned back happily in the wheel chair, and looked at the book in her lap until she just could not stand it any longer. Then slowly she opened it, and slowly turned all those unnecessary pages at the beginning until she reached the first story.

"Once upon a time," it said, invitingly — and off she went into it.

The fifth prince in the fifth story was up to

his ears in troubles when Amy heard a little waking-up cough from her parents' bedroom. She closed her book, patted it lovingly, laid it down, and hurried over to the door of the bedroom. Mama's eyes were open. She sat up in her bed, smiled at Amy, and beckoned. Amy moved quickly into the room.

"Do you think you can help me get up?" Mama whispered.

"Oh yes, sure I can," Amy said.

"What, what?" said Daddy, jumping up in his bed.

"Shh, shh, Harry," Mama said gently. "Don't get up. Go back to sleep now, go ahead. I'm fine."

Obediently, Daddy dropped back on his pillow.

Feeling very important, Amy walked over to the closet to fetch Mama her robe. She put out her hand for the heavy, navy-blue wool bathrobe, hesitated, made a face at it, and then reached all the way in the back of the closet where the beautiful yellow silk kimono hung. Aunt Janet had bought it for Mama while she was in the hospital, but Mama never seemed to wear it. Amy carried it over to the bed. Mama looked at it, started to say something, then smiled and slipped it on. Amy helped her on with her stockings, shoes, and brace. She brought the wheel chair over to the door of the bedroom, since it was too big to go through the narrow door, and with Mama leaning very heavily on her shoulder, carefully guided her over to it.

In a little while she and Mama were settled cozily in the kitchen, with the door closed. Even Aunt Minnie, usually an early bird, still slept.

It reminded Amy that long ago, every Saturday morning, she and Mama would get up early, before anybody else, and make pancakes. Nobody else in the family cared very much for pancakes, but Amy and Mama loved them. It was a special time for both of them. Mama would let Amy help mix the batter, and then the two of them would sit down to plates stacked high with smoking pancakes and eat as much as they wanted. Aunt Minnie made pancakes for Amy sometimes, but they always came out of a box and didn't really taste right. She hadn't eaten any of Mama's pancakes since the accident, and her eyes focused hopefully on Mama's face. Mama looked at her and grinned suddenly.

"Should we make our own breakfast today?" she whispered. "What would you like?"

"Pancakes!" Amy cried.

"I was hoping you'd say that," Mama laughed.

Amy felt so hungry suddenly that she could hardly wait. Quickly she bustled around fetching all the things Mama needed: flour, corn meal, baking powder, eggs, and milk. Mama rolled her wheel chair over to the table and began mixing. She looked happy. "It's good to be cooking again," she said.

When the batter was ready, Amy begged, "Please, Mama, let me make them."

Mama looked uncertain.

"Come on, Mama, please," Amy said. "I'm a big girl now, and I know how."

"I guess you'd have to anyway," Mama sighed, "but be careful."

Amy put the griddle on the stove, dropped a lump of butter onto it, and watched it melt away into foam. Mama told her to drop a tiny bit of water into the melted butter, and if it bounced, then the griddle was hot enough. The first drop of water just lay there, bubbling a little. But the second drop leaped all over the pan.

"Now!" said Mama.

Holding her breath, Amy spooned some of the batter onto the griddle. It formed a perfect circle. Carefully, she spooned three more pancakes beside it. Four handsome circles spluttered obediently. When the tops of the pancakes began to look holey, Amy slipped the spatula under the holeyest pancake and flipped. It went right over. Feeling as if she had been making pancakes all her life, she flipped the other three over and looked proudly down at them. All of them were a deep brown and looked like a turtle's shell, which is exactly how pancakes are supposed to look.

When they were done, she stacked them high on a plate and brought them to Mama.

"Why don't you have two, and I'll have two?" Mama suggested.

"No, no," Amy said briskly. "You eat these. The cook always gets to eat last."

She brought Mama the butter and syrup, and waited impatiently until Mama put the first bite into her mouth.

"Well?" she said anxiously.

Mama swallowed the piece quickly, looked at Amy, burst out laughing, and said, "Wonderful! As good as ever."

Sometimes it comes upon a person without any warning that whatever is happening at that moment has happened at some other time. It came upon Amy then that all this — the two of them sitting warm and contented in the cozy kitchen, eating pancakes, and Mama's happy voice saying "as good as ever" — had all taken place another time. Many other times. She felt a pang of loneliness because she had missed it so. And Mama had been gone for so long. Mama put another bite of pancake in her mouth, and then the loneliness was gone. It was all happening right now, and Mama was home, and they were eating pancakes, just the two of them, as they had done so many other Saturday mornings in the past.

"How about coffee?" Amy said, bursting with happiness. "I'll make you some coffee."

"I can wait till later," Mama said. "You make yourself some pancakes now."

"No, no," Amy insisted, "I know how to make coffee." She filled the coffee pot with six cups of water, dropped six tablespoons of coffee into it, and then an extra one for the pot. She put the pot on the stove and then looked at Mama again. Mama was eating her pancakes.

"Are they really good, Mama? Really?" Amy said. "You can tell me the truth."

Mama had a mouthful of pancakes so she just nodded her head vigorously, and said, "Mmmm!"

Suddenly Amy noticed that the table looked messy. The flour and all the other pancake ingredients were still standing there. That was no way for a table to look. She gathered up all the supplies and carried them over to the cupboard. Some of the flour spilled on the floor. She'd come back and clean it up in a minute. The table looked neater now, but —

"I'll be right back, Mama," she cried, hurrying out of the room. In a minute she was back with the vase of artificial roses from the living room. She placed it right in the middle of the kitchen table and stepped back to examine the effect.

"Lovely," Mama said. "It looks like a party."

"Party!" Amy cried. "Oh, Mama!" She pulled a chair over to the high shelves that held the fancy dishes, climbed up, and began fishing around inside. In a few minutes the two silver candlesticks were standing on either side of the vase, and Amy was poking around desperately in the closet under the sink.

"I think the candles are on the shelf with the furniture polish," Mama said, sounding excited too. "I hope we're not all out of them."

"I found them!" Amy yelled, holding up two partially used candles. She placed them in the holders, lit them, and studied the effect with a troubled frown.

"Too much light," she announced, and

turned off the kitchen light. Still it wasn't right, so she pulled down the window shade, and then looked with enchantment at the transformed room.

The coffee boiled over suddenly, and Amy raced over to the stove and turned off the flame. In the magical semidarkness, she brought Mama a cup of coffee.

"Now you make yourself some pancakes," Mama said dreamily, looking at the candles. "Better put the light on just while you're making them."

In a short time Amy was seated at the table, four smoking pancakes on the plate in front of her. The kitchen light was out, the candles glowed, and the hole in her stomach was overpowering.

"Candles always make me feel hungry," she said, pouring syrup over her pancakes, "but Aunt Minnie says that people who put candles on their table don't want you to see what the food looks like."

Mama giggled and sipped her coffee. "I like candles too," she confessed.

"Let's do this again next Saturday," Amy said, chewing rapturously on the pancakes. "Aren't these wonderful?" She finished her stack quickly and said, "How about some more? I'm still starving."

"So am I," Mama said. "I guess candles make me hungry too."

Suddenly the light went on and Daddy was standing there in the doorway, looking worried. "Hannah," he said, "I didn't know where you were. Why didn't you call me when you got up?"

"You were so tired, Harry," Mama said, blinking in the light. "But Amy helped me. I'm fine."

"You should have waited for me," Daddy insisted. "You could have fallen." He walked into the room, and looked down at her with a concerned look on his face.

"It's all right, Harry," Mama said, smiling. "We've been having a nice quiet breakfast, just the two of us."

"It's cold in here," Daddy said. "You're not dressed warmly enough. I'll bring you a sweater."

"I'm fine really," Mama insisted, but Daddy hurried out of the room. He returned in a minute with the sweater, followed by Aunt Minnie.

"What in the world!" Aunt Minnie exclaimed, looking at the candles, the vase, the flour on the floor, the spilled coffee on the stove, and the messy sink.

"We made pancakes," Amy said weakly.

"Well, why didn't you wait for me?" Aunt Minnie said sharply. "Just look at this mess!"

"I told her it would be all right," Mama said in a little voice. She and Amy exchanged guilty looks.

"Well, she shouldn't have bothered you," Aunt Minnie said gently to Mama, but she cast a meaningful look in Amy's direction. "You need all the rest you can get, and sometimes she can be a very thoughtless girl." She picked up a sponge and began mopping up the flour on the floor.

Laura hurried into the room, buttoning up a sweater, her face still puffy with sleep. She peered at the kitchen clock. "Nine thirty," she groaned. "I'm late. I was supposed to be there at nine o'clock." She started out of the kitchen.

"Where are you going, Laura?" Mama said.

"To Anne's."

"But it's pouring. She's the girl you met at camp, isn't she? And doesn't she live all the way down on Longfellow Avenue?"

"Uh huh." Laura moved impatiently in the doorway. "I'll wear my raincoat and take my umbrella."

"Well — have your breakfast first," Mama urged.

"I'm not hungry," Laura insisted. "I'll eat

112

at her house." She disappeared down the long hall.

"Laura — " Mama began.

"Oh, it's all right, Hannah," said Daddy. "Let her go. It's good for her to get out."

Aunt Minnie wrung the sponge out at the sink. "That's right," she said. "She used to sit around here all day with her nose in a book. You couldn't budge her."

Mama nodded, and looked down at her plate.

"Do you want any more pancakes, Mama?" Amy said hopefully. "How many should I make for you this time?" She walked over to the stove and lit the flame under the griddle.

"I guess I've had enough, darling," Mama said. "Go ahead and make some more for yourself."

Amy turned off the flame. "I guess I've had enough too," she said.

Aunt Minnie inspected the contents of the bowl. "Harry," she said, "I'll make you some pancakes."

"No thanks," Daddy said. "I'll just have some toast and coffee."

"There's enough batter here," Aunt Minnie said grimly, casting another meaningful look at Amy, "to feed an army."

"All right, I will have pancakes," Daddy said vaguely. "It's cold in here, Hannah, and you're sitting right near the window." He moved the wheel chair to the other end of the table. Mama didn't say anything, and her face looked very tired.

"It's my fault," Amy thought guiltily. "She's tired because of me. Aunt Minnie's right — why did I bother her? I should have known better."

"I'll go make my bed," she mumbled, and hurried out of the room.

Laura was just opening the outside door as Amy came up the hall.

"Oh Laura," she said, "I have to talk to you about something."

"Later," Laura said, and rushed out the door.

Amy walked into the living room, stopped, and thought about whether she should go and cry in the bathroom or in her bedroom.

The *Olive Fairy Book* was still lying on the coffee table. She picked it up, opened to the story she had been reading, and flopped into the green arm chair.

Then a miracle happened. Samba the coward, the skulker, the terrified, no sooner found himself pressed hard, unable to escape, than something sprang into life within him and he fought with all his might. . . .

Amy took a deep breath. From now on, she would just have to try and be more considerate of Mama, and as the bright, comforting words of the story enveloped her, she forgot all about crying.

# Bicycles

Early the next morning, Laura hurried along the street, a grim smile on her face. Thank goodness she had managed to get out of the house before Daddy had a chance to corner her on the stoop. She was so tired of those lectures on the stoop, tired of listening to all the things she was doing wrong, tired of creeping around the house with that silly smile on her face, tired of Mama worrying about everything she did. "Wear a sweater, Laura, you'll catch cold." "Be careful when you cross the street." "Don't carry all those books — they're too heavy."

Every time she looked at Mama sitting in that horrible wheel chair, she felt like crying. She knew it wasn't Mama's fault, and she felt guilty at the terrible thoughts that never seemed to leave her. But when she was home she never seemed to say anything or do anything that was right. The best thing was for her to stay out of the house as much as possible.

She hurried across the street, jingled the coins in her pocket, and tried to think of something pleasant. She and Anne were going biking today, and the only enjoyable part of the whole prospect was that she would be seeing her friend again. She had never ridden a bike before, and the thought of that was not especially appealing. Yesterday, because of the rain, she and Anne had spent the whole day indoors at Anne's house. They had played checkers mostly, which Laura loved, particularly since she was now able to beat Anne at least fifty per cent of the time. But Anne hated being in for very long, and had insisted that they go biking today if the weather turned good. Unfortunately it had.

"Hey, you!" somebody shouted behind her.

Laura turned. It was Veronica Ganz. "Hi," she said, and waited for Veronica to catch up.

There was nobody else out on the street except for a small boy who was walking some distance behind Veronica. Laura's hand closed uncertainly over the coins in her pocket.

"Where you been?" Veronica demanded. "How come you're not on the up staircase any more?"

"I'm not a monitor any more," Laura said painfully.

"How come?"

"My mother," Laura began. She looked up

into Veronica's face, and her fingers loosened over the coins. How good it would be to tell somebody all her troubles!

Suddenly Veronica whirled around and shouted, "Go home, Stanley!"

The little boy stopped walking and stood motionless.

"Stanley, I'll break your neck," Veronica screamed, and took a few running steps in his direction.

Stanley retreated a few steps back and stood warily on his toes. He said nothing, but Laura could see how intently he kept his eyes on Veronica.

Veronica shook her fist at him, looked back at Laura, made two stamping steps in his direction (Stanley swayed slightly but held his ground), and then returned to Laura.

"Come on, let's walk fast," she commanded, grabbing Laura's arm.

"I'm going this way," Laura protested as Veronica tried to head her in a different direction.

"Where you going?"

"Biking."

"Good," said Veronica, "let's go."

"I'm meeting my friend," Laura said uncomfortably.

"Who is she?"

"Nobody you know. She doesn't go to P.S.

118

63," Laura said quickly, and then changing the subject she asked, "Who's that little boy?"

"My brother," Veronica hissed. "The brat! He follows me everywhere I go."

"I thought you only had a sister," Laura said.

"He's just a half-brother. What's your friend's name?"

"Anne."

"Anne what?"

"Anne Sherman," Laura said, wishing now that Veronica would go away.

"That's a stupid name," Veronica said, wrinkling up her face sullenly. "Anyway, why aren't you a monitor any more? I keep looking for you, and now they have that fat jerk standing there all the time. Yesterday I stepped on her foot, and she tried to act like she didn't even see me."

A warm, contented feeling spread inside Laura, and she looked appreciatively at Veronica. Linda Briansky was the name of the girl who had taken over Laura's post. She certainly was fat, and probably a jerk, and Laura hated her with all her heart. Every time she passed Linda going up the stairs and saw her acting so important, and heard her ordering everybody to "Hurry it up!" or "Get in line there!" she felt like crying.

She smiled gratefully at Veronica and said

weakly, "She's only doing what she's supposed to do."

"Baloney!" said Veronica.

They walked along silently for a while.

"Your name's Laura, isn't it?" Veronica said softly.

"Uh huh."

"Laura Stern?"

"That's right."

"My name is Veronica. Veronica Ganz."

"I know that," Laura said in surprise.

"Oh! I thought you did, but I wasn't sure."

The bicycle store was across the street, and just around the corner. Laura stopped walking and said, "Well, I guess I better say goodbye now."

Veronica stopped walking, and Stanley, bringing up the rear, also stopped. Veronica looked down at her feet and said, "I can ride a bike real good. You should see me. I can even ride backwards."

"Well —" Laura said uncertainly. Her eyes settled on Stanley. Even at a distance she could see that his nose was running.

"His nose is running."

"Whose nose is running?"

"Your brother's. Stanley's."

"Stanley!" Veronica shouted, turning to look at him, "Wipe your nose."

Stanley drew his sleeve across his face. "Oooh!" Laura grimaced.

"Wait till I get you," Veronica cried. "Just wait! I'll smack you so hard you won't know what hit you. I'll teach you to follow me. I'll — " She darted toward him, and Laura said quietly, "Well, good-bye, Veronica."

She hurried across the street and began walking quickly, hoping that Veronica would not follow her. She breathed a sigh of relief as she turned the corner and saw Anne standing there in front of the store. Anne smiled as Laura came hurrying up and said, "Your hat's on backward."

Anne's hat, a red corduroy skullcap with a feather in it, fitted her perfectly. So did her red corduroy jacket and plaid skirt. She was just Laura's height, with the same color hair and eyes, but there, Laura reflected, the resemblance ended. Anne was so pretty, and so slim too.

"Come on, let's go," Anne said, walking into the bicycle store.

Inside, she walked up and down, casting a knowing eye over the waiting bikes. There were two categories. You could hire a bike for twenty-five cents an hour or for thirty-five cents an hour. If you simply wanted to ride a bike, you chose a twenty-five cent one. But if you not only wanted to ride a bike, but also to be followed by jealous and admiring glances, you chose a thirty-five-cent one.

Gleaming with chrome and fresh paint, some with rabbit tails hanging from their backs and horns on their fronts, the thirty-five-cent bikes stood proudly beside their humble relations. Laura looked at them with admiration, but Anne put her hands on two quiet, modest-looking bikes.

"How much money have you got?" she asked.

"Fifty cents."

"Me too. Let's see. Twenty-five cents for the first hour, ten cents for every hour after that. Mmmm. Three and a half hours. It's eleven o'clock now. We have to be back by two thirty."

They pushed their bikes across the street to the bicycle path in Crotona Park. Then Anne mounted her bicycle and whizzed off down the path. She dipped first to one side, then the other, did fancy turns, held on with one hand, then with none, and made the simple little bike look as if it had wings. It all seemed so easy, too. Laura put one leg across her bike, and realized right away that it would not be easy.

In a little while Anne was back. She jumped

off the bike while it was still in motion, and then propped it against a tree.

"Okay," she said, "I'll show you how, and then we'll ride together."

She held the bike while Laura mounted it.

"Now just relax," she urged, and began moving the bike. Laura held onto the handlebars as tightly as she could, and stared down in terror at the front wheel.

"Now," said Anne, running alongside and still holding the bike, "just start riding." She gave the bike a powerful push and let go, and Laura immediately went down sideways, with the bike on top of her.

"No, no, no!" Anne lectured, helping her up. "You're not doing it right. Just ride. That's all you have to do. Just ride."

She got Laura up on the seat once more, ran alongside holding on, and then let go.

This time Laura fell off the bike and skinned her knee.

"That's not the right way," Anne said, helping her up again. "There's nothing to it. Just ride. That's all. When my father showed me how, I did it right away."

"The wheels don't turn right," Laura suggested helplessly. "Maybe something's wrong with the bike."

"No, it's you," Anne laughed. "The wheels

won't turn right unless your feet turn them. Look!" She hopped on Laura's bike and flew off, executing the same effortless feats as she had on her own bike.

"See how you do it?" she said when she returned.

Arabella O'Brien, who was in Laura's class, came along just then.

"Hi, Laura," she said.

"Oh hi!"

Arabella watched as Anne got Laura up on the bike, started off with her, let go, and then ran over to pick Laura and the bike off the ground.

"Say," she said to Anne, "is that your bike over there?"

"Uh huh."

"Could I ride it for a while?"

"I guess so," Anne said, "but come right back."

Laura watched Arabella whizz off on Anne's bike, and decided to give up right now and stop wasting Anne's time. But Anne kept insisting. By the time Arabella came back, Laura had skinned her other knee and torn her jacket.

"Why don't you give me a hand with her?" Anne said to Arabella, panting and red in the face now. "If you hold her up on one side, I'll hold her up on the other."

But no good came of this maneuver either. Laura's feet remained glued to the pedals, her hands gripped the handlebars, her balance was off, and her eyes fixed themselves in terror down on the front wheel.

So Arabella took another turn on Anne's bike. She stayed away a little longer this time; and when she returned, Helen Franklin and Juanita Peterson, both in her class, had joined Anne and were lumbering along with Laura propped on her bike in the center. After a few more flops, Helen, who had brought her own bike, and Juanita, on Anne's bike, went off for a short spin.

"I don't know — you're just not trying," Anne said crossly. Suddenly noticing a figure on a bicycle some distance away, she started shouting, "Hey, John, Jo-ohn, John-ee!"

The figure heard, raised one hand easily in greeting, and skimmed over to her side.

"Hi, Anne," said John. He was a redhaired, handsome boy, and Laura noticed that he looked at Anne as if he liked what he saw.

"Hi, John. This is my friend Laura. Laura — John."

"Hi." For a brief moment, John allowed his eyes to light on Laura's face, and then, smiling, turned back to Anne.

"I didn't know you ever came here," he said happily.

"Say, John," Anne asked, "will you give me a hand with Laura? I'm trying to teach her to ride."

"Sure," said John agreeably. He got off his bike, but before he could lay it down, Arabella asked if she could ride it for a while.

"Sure," said John.

He and Anne surrounded Laura, got her going, let go, and watched the bike flop over on top of her.

"Look, Anne," Laura said, "this is stupid. You're not doing any riding at all. Let's stop for a while. Please! You go ahead and ride."

"All right, just for a little while. John can stay and help you," Anne said, obviously knowing that her wishes would be obeyed.

She signaled to Juanita, but Helen came whizzing back instead.

"Here, take my bike," Helen said. "Juanita wants to ride a little longer."

So Anne rode off on Helen's bike. John stood silently for a moment, watching Anne as she grew smaller and smaller. Then he turned and looked at Laura. His face grew businesslike.

"Let's go," he ordered.

Laura staggered over to the bike. "I can't do it," she mumbled, "I just can't."

"Just get on," said John. Now that he

wasn't watching Anne, he was free to devote his full attention to Laura.

"Don't look down at the wheel," John said. "That's why your balance is off. Come on now, look up. That's right."

Laura looked up at a tree not too far off. John started pushing her bike, let go, and then — suddenly — she was riding, really riding, all by herself. Straight off she went on the bike, straight, straight, straight — into the tree.

Her nose was scratched, but her heart was joyful. She could hardly wait to ride again. John helped her up, started her off, and there she went again — really riding, all by herself. She could hear John running behind her, shouting encouraging remarks. The wind blew in her face, the wheels hummed, and she rode. But then, on the other side of the path, Juanita Peterson, riding Anne's bike, came whizzing along from the other direction. There was quite a distance between them, but Laura's eyes fastened themselves helplessly on Juanita, and the obedient bike followed. Crash! Juanita, and Laura lay wrapped up in the two bikes.

"No, no," John said, helping her up. "Don't keep looking at one thing, or you'll go into it. Always look away at something else, and you won't have any trouble."

127

"Let's go! Let's go!" Laura cried, eager to be off again.

John only had to give her a little push this time, and off she went. Oh, it was wonderful being able to ride! Thrilling, beautiful, glorious to fly over the ground with the wind. Anne passed her, going the other way, and as Laura felt her bike wobble, she looked straight ahead, and nothing happened. She circled the path without any mishap, but then, halfway around the second time, a little boy chasing a ball, ran into the path in front of her. Quickly, she looked to one side. The bike followed. Off the path she flew, down a bumpy earth field, across a path, down another field, and there at the bottom, coming closer all the time, was Indian Lake. Oh — help! Her hands froze on the handlebars, her feet on the pedals. In terror, her eyes never left the lake growing closer and closer all the time. Behind her, somebody was shouting. John. Yes, yes! She knew — look away — quick. She turned her head and looked violently to one side, and the bike responded. Missing Indian Lake by about a yard, the bike veered suddenly and whammed into a park attendant who was innocently picking up pieces of paper with his pointed stick.

Aside from a bruised eye, a banged elbow,

and an earful of pointed remarks about stupid kids who don't look where they're going, Laura rose unscathed and joyful from the ground.

The rest of the afternoon passed in a whirl of glory. She learned to start herself off and to use the foot brake. She still couldn't turn very well, but that would come another time. Lots of other children joined them on the bicycle path, and except for a few minor crack-ups, Laura also learned to maneuver her bike around other bikes. Another world was born for her that afternoon — a world of speed, and wind, and excitement. A world in which no unpleasant thoughts could possibly enter.

Nobody had a watch, and Anne had to suggest, and then urge, and finally insist that they return their bikes. "It must be nearly two thirty," she said, as she finally got Laura moving in the direction of the store. Halfway there, Anne said suddenly to Laura, "Didn't you have a blue bike?"

Laura looked down at the red bicycle she was pushing and tried to think clearly out of the clouds of glory that still surrounded her.

"Yes, I think I did," she said slowly.

"Well — what happened to it?"

"Oh," Laura groaned, "Gloria Fernback

asked me if she could ride mine, and then I tried Helen Franklin's, and then Arabella — "

"Come on, let's go back," Anne sighed. "You're really a bonehead today."

But when they arrived back at the park, Gloria Fernbach was riding Jacqueline Shapiro's bike and Arabella had gone home. Finally Juanita Peterson turned up on Laura's bike, and then they had to find Helen Franklin, who was riding Gloria Fernbach's bike.

The clock in the bicycle store said four fifteen, and Jack, the owner of Jack's Bicycles and Motorcycles, was not especially sympathetic. Laura gave him her name and address, and promised to come back tomorrow with the thirty-five cents still owing for herself and Anne.

"It's my fault we were late," she insisted when Anne offered to pay her back seventeen and a half cents.

The girls parted on Boston Road and agreed to go riding again on Tuesday afternoon, weather permitting, money available, and parents agreeable.

As she limped back home through the darkening streets, Laura's bruised eye began to puff up. Her nose felt raw and swollen, the scrapes on her knees and elbows were stinging, and a deep Charley horse was beginning to tighten around her thighs. But she felt gloriously lightheaded, and it was not until she dragged herself through the door of her house and found Mama and Daddy sitting in the living room that her happiness began to evaporate.

"Laura," Mama gasped, "what happened to you?"

"Nothing, nothing," Laura said, trying to smile reassuringly. "I'm fine. I've just been learning to ride a bike. That's all."

"You?" Daddy said, "learning to ride a bike? *You?*"

"Yes, me," Laura said in a hurt voice. "Why not me?"

Daddy grinned. "I'm just surprised. I never thought you were interested in biking."

"I am now," Laura said.

"But just look at her," Mama cried. "She's hurt. Where did you go? What happened to you?"

"To the park," Laura said quickly. "The bicycle path there. It's safe. There aren't any cars. I'm going again Tuesday."

"But you're full of bruises," Mama said. "It's not safe."

Laura said tensely, "I fell a lot today because I didn't know how to ride. But now I do, and I won't fall any more after this."

"Lots of children ride bikes," Daddy said to Mama. "The bicycle path is safe, and I think it's good for her to ride. But if you're going to worry about it, Hannah —"

"If she's going to worry about it" — Laura thought rebelliously to herself. "She worries about everything I do."

"It's just that she's not the type of child who's good at sports," Mama said. "Remember what happened when she tried to roller-skate — how she nearly broke her arm? And that time she fell off the scooter?"

"People change," Laura burst out. "I'm a different person now than I used to be, and —" Desperately, she shut her mouth and swallowed the words that were rushing out. "You're different too," she thought unhappily. "You've changed too. You're not the same person you used to be."

"It's up to you, Hannah," Daddy said, casting a warning look at Laura. "Whatever you say."

Mama said slowly, "I wouldn't want to stop her from doing something she really enjoys, but —"

"I really enjoy it," Laura cried.

Mama looked nervously at her. "So many terrible things can happen if you're not careful —"

"I'll be careful!" Laura hurried out of the room before Mama could say anything else. She couldn't bear it this time if Mama said "No." That tormenting thought grew inside her again, and she tried desperately to stifle it. But there it was just the same, and Laura dropped on the bed and buried her face in the pillow to escape from it. But it followed her there and whispered to her that, bad as everything had been when Mama was away, it was worse now that she was home.

# My Best Friend

Amy sat shivering on the park bench and wished it would snow. Maybe then Laura would stay home and a person could have a chance to talk to her. With loathing, her eyes sifted through the bicycle riders on the path and finally settled on Laura, riding along on Helen Franklin's bike. She watched as Laura dipped the bike first to one side, then to the other, and executed a one-hand turn.

"Show-off!" she grumbled to herself.

Laura certainly had it bad, this bicycle fever. Every afternoon for the past couple of weeks she had spent most of her time here. She'd used up all the money in her bank, spent her allowance, and still came, hogging rides from children who had bikes. It was disgusting, that's what it was, Amy thought loftily, to hang around, begging people to lend you their bikes. Mama didn't like it either, even though she hadn't exactly told Laura to stop. But it was very selfish of Laura, anyway, not to show a little more consideration for Mama's feelings.

Helen Franklin was seated a few benches

away, talking to Gloria Fernbach. Amy thought for a moment and then got up and walked over to them.

"Hi, Helen," she said, wrapping her arms around herself. "Isn't it freezing?"

"I guess so," Helen said.

"Nearly time to go home," continued Amy, "it'll be dark soon."

"No it won't," Helen said mildly, "not for another hour or so."

Amy returned to her own bench. She watched Laura trying to make a turn with both hands off the handlebars. The bicycle began to spin, and Laura fell over. "Good for her!" Amy thought savagely.

She watched hopefully as Laura brought the bike back to Helen. Maybe now. "Laura," Amy called, rising and walking over to her, "are you ready now?"

Laura looked at her with that irritating, faraway look in her eyes. "Soon, soon," she said, and turned and hurried over to Roslyn Beckerman, who was riding Gloria Fernbach's bike.

Amy sat down on the bench again and watched Laura whizz away on Gloria's bike. A hopeless sense of terror rose inside of her. If Laura didn't help her, she would be lost. Because today Mrs. Malucci had remembered. Early that morning she had said to the class, "Some of you children have not handed in all the assignments. Don't think that because I haven't said anything to you, it means I've forgotten. I'm just not going to waste any time telling you something you already know. Next week, when the report cards come around, you'll see very clearly that I didn't forget."

Amy immediately understood that Mrs. Malucci's remarks were directed entirely toward her. She worried about it the whole day, and that afternoon, after the other children left, she lingered at the teacher's desk.

"Well?" said Mrs. Malucci.

"I just wanted to explain, Mrs. Malucci," Amy said with a plaintive note in her voice, "why I didn't hand in that 'My Best Friend' composition yet."

"What 'My Best Friend' composition?" said Mrs. Malucci.

"The one I didn't hand in," Amy explained quickly. "You see, my mother was away in the hospital, and she came home the night I was supposed to write it, and — " She looked up into Mrs. Malucci's face, hoping that her reference to Mama's being in the hospital might move her to show mercy.

"How is your mother now?" asked Mrs. Malucci, not looking particularly merciful.

"Oh, better, I guess," Amy continued, "but

I wanted you to know why I didn't hand it in."

"Well, get it in by tomorrow," Mrs. Malucci said firmly, turning back to the work on her desk.

Amy stood there watching her, and then suddenly, without even realizing what she was doing, she blurted out, "Do you have five children or six children?"

Mrs. Malucci looked at her steadily with those watery gray eyes and answered, "I have six children, and two grandchildren." Then she put a hand on Amy's arm and said, "I hope your mother will be able to come next week during Open School Week. I'd like to discuss your work with her."

Amy had a pretty good idea what *that* meant, and quickly grabbed her books and hurried off. Oh, why had she asked Mrs. Malucci such an impudent question? Why was she always putting her foot in her mouth? Weren't things bad enough as they were? Didn't Mrs. Malucci already dislike her more than anybody else in the class? Rosa got to water the plants, Cynthia washed the blackboards, Annette de Luca cleaned the board erasers, but Amy Stern got only criticism and extra work. Ever since she had read *Oliver Twist* for a book report, and handed in a poem instead of an ordinary composition,

Mrs. Malucci had been piling more and more work on her. She had thought Mrs. Malucci might even like the poem. What a dope she had been! Mrs. Malucci kept sending her to the library for special assignments that nobody else had to do. Mrs. Malucci made her read books — crazy books like *Lorna Doone* and *The Cricket on the Hearth* — and write extra book reports about them. And Mrs. Malucci never was satisfied. No matter how hard she worked — and in all her school life she had never worked harder — Mrs. Malucci always found something to criticize. Her punctuation, her grammar, her penmanship — something was always wrong.

The second report-card period would be coming up next week, and Amy shuddered to think of it. The first time she had received a B in conduct and a B in work, which were pretty standard marks that had followed her throughout her school career. But this time! She knew she was getting a C in conduct. She could thank Laura for that. But what if she got a C in work, or even a D? Her eyes began to fill with tears.

What would Mama say if she brought home a report card that had a C or a D in work? Maybe Daddy ought to go and talk to Mrs. Malucci, and explain how important it was for Mama to hear only good news and see only cheerful sights. Like a report card with an A in conduct and an A in work. Daddy might even point out to Mrs. Malucci that a bad report card might just result in a relapse for Mama. As it was, lately Mama had been more tired and sort of serious, even though all of them tried to laugh and tell her funny stories. Maybe it was because she knew something was wrong at school. Maybe she was worrying about how badly Amy was doing. Amy felt a pang of guilt. Of course she hadn't told Mama any of the real details about Mrs. Malucci. She had been very careful about that. Maybe once or twice she had let a few things slip about all the extra work she had to do. And she had mentioned the "My Best Friend" composition a few times. But Mama hadn't seemed upset at all. She had only said that Amy should do the best she could and that nobody could expect more than that.

Nobody but Mrs. Malucci. So perhaps it would be better not to have Daddy say anything to her. Perhaps the best thing for Mama would be for Laura to write the composition for her, which was why she was sitting here freezing in the first place.

And nobody could say she hadn't tried. Why, she had been worrying about that composition for weeks now; and with all the time

139

she'd been putting in on her homework and the extra assignments, she'd had hardly any time left to play. Never in her whole life had she done so much schoolwork by herself as she had since this term started. And whose fault was it really? Mrs. Malucci's? No, not completely. It was a fifty-fifty proposition, and Laura was as much to blame for all her misery as Mrs. Malucci.

Because all of a sudden Laura had abandoned her. That's just what she had done — deserted her — in cold blood. It was never like this in the old days. All the maps, the arithmetic problems, the book reports Laura had "helped" on. All she ever had to do was ask, or cry a little if Laura was being virtuous that day, and Laura would sit right down and get to work. Nothing was impossible when Laura helped, because Laura might be a stinker, but she was also the smartest person that Amy had ever met. But lately every time she asked Laura to help, Laura was always rushing off someplace or busy with her own homework.

Amy's foot fell asleep, so she stood up and gloomily began stamping it. Helen Franklin mounted her bike, waved to her friends, and began riding out of the park. This was an encouraging sign. Amy's foot woke up and she stopped stamping. Then Gloria Fernbach called something to Laura, who was doing figure eights on her bike. Laura stopped and rode the bike over to Gloria.

"Will you be here tomorrow?" Amy heard Laura ask.

"Yup," said Gloria, and rode away.

Amy hurried over to Laura and took her arm. "Are you coming home now?" she pleaded.

Laura cast a hungry eye around the bicycle path. The ranks had thinned. Only a couple of boys remained as the evening began settling down around them. "I guess so," Laura sighed.

Amy took a firm hold on Laura's arm and began propelling her out of the park.

"You've got to help me, Laura," she said desperately. "If I don't get that composition in by tomorrow, I don't know what she'll do to me."

"What who'll do to you?" Laura murmured dreamily.

"Mrs. Malucci!" Amy cried.

"Oh — what does she want you to do?" Laura's voice still sounded far away.

Amy began to cry. "You're not interested in me any more," she sobbed. "You never help me any more. You don't care what happens to me."

Completely overcome by a hopeless sense

of abandonment, Amy sat down on the curb. Her shoulders heaving with sobs, she buried her face in her hands and wept. In a second, Laura's arms were around her, and Laura's comforting voice broke through the misery. "Don't cry, Amy. Don't cry, bunny. Come on now, tell Laura all about it."

This was more like it. Amy sank her head gratefully on Laura's shoulder, and cried a while longer while Laura kissed her and patted her shoulder and waited for the tears to stop.

They stayed where they were, sitting on the curb, their arms around each other while Amy reviewed all the details about the "My Best Friend" composition.

"Well, what's the problem?" Laura said finally. "Rosa's your best friend, isn't she?"

Amy was silent.

"Don't tell me," Laura said with a note of horror in her voice, "that you think that drip Cynthia is your best friend?"

Amy sighed. "No," she admitted. "I guess she's not. But sometimes," she continued feebly, "I think she is."

Laura shook her head tolerantly. "You're just not very bright," she said. "But all right. Even if you don't realize that Rosa is your best friend — and what she sees in you I don't know — you could always say in the composition that you can't decide between the two of them. And then describe both of them."

"I thought of doing that," Amy admitted sadly, "but that's not right either."

"Look," Laura said kindly, "just stop worrying about it. I'll help you with it tonight, and we'll say that we — I mean you — just can't make up your mind. Okay? Feel better now?" She squeezed Amy's shoulder affectionately, and for one brief, lovely second Amy felt the heavy weight of indecision begin to evaporate. But only for a second.

"No," she groaned, "she'd know I didn't write it myself. She knows everything."

"Oh, we'll make it sound like you," Laura said heartily. "We'll leave out all the commas, and spell a few things wrong, and use little words."

"No, no," cried Amy, "but it wouldn't be what I mean."

"What do you mean, it wouldn't be what you mean?" Laura said impatiently.

"I mean she's wrong to make me write something I can't write. I mean some things you can't make a person say. Some things aren't right if you say them."

Out of the dusk in the street that lay before

them, a silver bike ridden by a silent, silver rider flew past them. Laura's eyes left Amy's face and followed in its path.

"Maybe so," she murmured dreamily again. "Some things you can't say. I know what you mean. Like that." She waved an arm after the disappearing figure. Then she turned to Amy, and said softly, "Why don't you say that?"

"Say what?"

"Say that you can't say it. What you just said. Some things aren't right if you say them."

And suddenly Amy couldn't wait to get home and begin writing her composition. Because now it was all right in her mind. What she would say. What she couldn't say.

She threw her arms around Laura's neck and plastered kisses all over her cheeks. "Laura," she said, laughing, "I love you so much. What would I do without you? I couldn't get along without you."

"I know, I know," Laura said smugly, laughing. She stood up, pulled Amy to her feet, and with their arms entwined around each other, they began walking home. On the way, Amy poured out all her other troubles with Mrs. Malucci into Laura's attentive ear. When she got to the part about all the special reports and *Lorna Doone* and *The Cricket*

144

*on the Hearth*, Laura stopped walking, a troubled frown on her face.

"Now why is she making you do all that?" she said.

"Because she hates me."

Laura took a long, uneasy look at her sister's face. "Sometimes when a teacher loads somebody up with work like that, it means —

"What?"

"It means," Laura continued slowly, "that she might think you're smart."

Amy snorted, and when Laura heard that snort and saw the dirty, tear-stained, skinny little face looking up at her, the frown faded.

"What am I thinking of?" she laughed. "Let's get home. I'm starving."

All evening long, Amy worked on her composition. She used both sides of five pages to tell Mrs. Malucci what she couldn't say. The composition started this way:

MY BEST FRIEND

Sometimes people ask you a question that you can't answer. Like who is your best friend? People should understand that sometimes you can't say what you are feeling. Sometimes when I try to be friendly to someone, and that person is mean to me, I know what it feels like. It feels bad. But that word "bad" is not the way it feels. I don't know what it feels like, but it isn't bad, and I don't know how to say what it is. . . .

The composition went on to tell of the many things that were impossible to describe. Amy discovered as she wrote that there was no end to the feelings that she couldn't write about. Like the way chicken-noodle soup tastes when you are sick, the way you feel when you read a beautiful fairy tale or see a dead cat lying in the street. After five pages of describing all the things that could not be described, Amy ended her composition.

She didn't show it to Laura. She didn't even want to show it to Laura. Because it was absolutely right the way it was, and she didn't want anybody, not even Laura, to suggest any changes. She knew Mrs. Malucci wouldn't like it. She knew Mrs. Malucci would find a hundred and one things wrong with it, but she didn't care. Because it was exactly what she had meant all along.

# Open School Week

When Aunt Minnie walked into Laura's classroom on Wednesday morning of Open School Week, Laura rose from her seat, walked over to her aunt, and escorted her to Mrs. Foster. The other children pulled out their arithmetic books and began working on homework problems.

"Mrs. Foster," Laura recited, "may I present my aunt, Mrs. Karnovsky. My mother is not able to come."

"I'm sorry your mother couldn't come," Mrs. Foster said, "but I'm certainly pleased to meet you, Mrs. Karnovsky. I hope you won't be shocked at all the terrible things I have to say about Laura." She beamed at Aunt Minnie, and Aunt Minnie beamed at her. Laura dropped her eyes modestly as both adults shifted their gaze to her.

"You may be seated now, dear," Mrs. Foster said pleasantly, and Laura turned and began walking back to her seat. She could feel her heart pounding away under her starched white blouse. Every girl in the class was wearing a white blouse today, even though it wasn't Friday, Assembly Day. And every boy, except for Leonard Rosenkranz, was wearing a white shirt and tie. Mrs. Foster had said earlier that week how nice it would be if they all could dress in white shirts and blouses on the day the parents came to visit — "as a mark of respect."

But there was Leonard Rosenkranz, in the fourth seat of the fifth row, wearing an awful-looking blue plaid shirt and no tie. And it wasn't because he did not own a white shirt and tie, either. The teachers were always very careful to point out that if you didn't own a white shirt or blouse, you shouldn't feel bad about spoiling the appearance of the class, and nobody should make fun of you either. But Leonard Rosenkranz did have a white shirt and tie, and he hadn't been absent on the day Mrs. Foster had urged them all to dress up for the occasion.

Leonard must have suddenly become aware of Laura's interest in his shirt, for he lifted his head from his desk and crossed his eyes at her. Loftily, Laura turned her head away, and before sitting down, glanced quickly at the chalk mural on the back blackboard. The class had been working on it for the past few weeks, and it certainly looked impressive. The face of every American President had been drawn in colored chalks by the students in Laura's class. Since there were thirty-seven children in the class, two children had to double up. Laura had worked with Howard Cummings on the face of Ulysses S. Grant. Thank goodness Howard knew how to make whiskers. The best face was Benjamin Harrison's, which was not surprising, since Nancy Hadlock, the outstanding artist in the class, had worked on him. The worst, naturally was Thomas Jefferson, done by Leonard Rosenkranz.

Laura sat down, laid her arithmetic book on the desk, and stole a curious look up front. Mrs. Foster and Aunt Minnie were still smiling at each other, and Mrs. Foster was talking. Unfortunately, Laura sat near the back of the room, and Mrs. Foster was speaking so softly that she couldn't hear a thing. But judging from the smiles, there could be no doubt as to the nature of Mrs. Foster's remarks. After all, Laura thought smugly as she began filling in the heading on her homework paper, this was her fourteenth Open School Week, and with the exception of Miss Potter in 5B, no teacher had ever found anything to criticize in her work.

Laura's eyes narrowed as she remembered Miss Potter and the old, nearly forgotten sense of bewilderment at Miss Potter's dislike for her. Why? Miss Potter was young, pretty, liked by nearly all the children in the class, and evidently liked all the children too — except Laura. Miss Potter was not mean or strict, and yet she seldom missed a chance to humiliate Laura.

"You didn't write that composition yourself! Who did it for you?" She could still remember the time Miss Potter had insisted, in front of the whole class, that Laura was not telling the truth, and the icy look in her pretty blue eyes.

And yet her work had been as good as usual. She made 100 on most of her test papers. But often, when she got up to recite, Miss Potter would say, "Try not to sound like the encyclopedia, Laura. Just answer the question."

Mama had listened to all her troubles, comforted her, but done nothing until Open School Week. Laura squirmed with embarrassment as she remembered the interview. Not that she could hear anything that was said, but there were no smiles that time, and Mama had done most of the talking — angry talking, even though it was in whispers, that hissed across the quiet classroom. Laura could remember how her classmates had turned to look at her, and how she had tried not to cry through the confusion — and the pride, too.

But that was the only time Open School Week had been unpleasant. All the other twelve times Mama had stood listening, a proud smile on her face, as Laura's teachers praised her work. And this was the first time Mama had not come. Mama was home now, sitting in the wheel chair, waiting to hear what had been said. Laura frowned, and started doodling on her homework paper. What did it feel like, sitting in a wheel chair and waiting?

The door opened, and Marjorie Kahn's mother, followed by Leonard Rosenkranz's mother, entered the room. Mrs. Foster smiled at them, finished what she was saying to Aunt Minnie, and waved hospitably toward the back of the room. She was inviting Aunt Minnie to inspect the mural, and then to remain for a while and see the students at their work. Aunt Minnie nodded yes, fished her glasses out of her purse, and walked to the back of the room. Laura had mentioned several times to her that Ulysses S. Grant was the President she had drawn. But Aunt Minnie glanced quickly at Ulysses S. Grant, and then appeared terribly interested in James Madison and Herbert Hoover. Laura glanced over her shoulder a number of times, but was disappointed each time to find Aunt Minnie nowhere in the vicinity of Ulysses S. Grant.

151

Why did grownups always seem so interested in everybody else's work?

Mrs. Foster spoke with Marjorie Kahn's mother first, and there were more smiles all around. Marjorie was also a good student, so it was not surprising. After Marjorie Kahn's mother joined Aunt Minnie at the mural, Mrs. Foster began speaking with Leonard Rosenkranz's mother. It was immediately apparent to everybody in the class that this conversation would be somewhat different from the two that had gone before. First of all, Mrs. Foster looked serious. Then, instead of talking to Mrs. Rosenkranz at the side of her desk, as she had with the others, she led her outside into the hall.

The interview lasted long enough for Aunt Minnie and Mrs. Kahn to finish their inspection of the mural. Marjorie Kahn's mother didn't seem terribly interested in James Polk, whom Marjorie had drawn. Instead, she spent a lot of time admiring Ulysses S. Grant, while Aunt Minnie smiled over James Polk. Both of them finally sat down next to each other in the last seats of the fifth and sixth rows, and nodded pleasantly at all the children who kept turning to look at them.

When Mrs. Foster returned with Mrs. Rosenkranz, Mrs. Rosenkranz had a thoughtful look on her face. Everybody watched as she purposely walked down the fifth row, on her way to the mural. Leonard's eyes were glued to his work, but everybody saw Mrs. Rosenkranz halt briefly by the side of his desk, and everybody heard quite clearly the one whispered word she addressed to him. "Wait!" she said, and strode on to the back.

Mrs. Foster cleared her throat and suggested that the class work some of their arithmetic problems on the board. She called on Laura, Marjorie, Jack Lazarus, Emily Rawlings, and Leonard Rosenkranz. She naturally assumed that each parent would be interested in the work of her own child, and Emily Rawlings and Jack Lazarus, both excellent students, could be counted on not to make any embarrassing mistakes. Laura finished her problem first. "Very good," Mrs. Foster said, smiling. Laura walked back to her seat, stealing one quick little look at Aunt Minnie, who smiled and nodded. Emily, Marjorie, and Jack finished right behind her. "Very good," Mrs. Foster repeated. Leonard lingered at the board.

In a very sweet voice, without any of the irritation that generally punctuated all her conversations with Leonard, Mrs. Foster said, "Just find the least common denominator, dear."

But Leonard was unable to find it anywhere. After Mrs. Foster provided nearly every clue, Leonard finally discovered it, and after some more suggestions from his teacher, finished the problem and returned to his seat.

"Very good," said Mrs. Foster.

She talked for a little while about fractions, and then it was time for music. The children put away their books, stood up, faced the window, and stretched once — "Hands down!" — twice — "Hands down!" — three times. Everybody sat down, and watched Mrs. Foster draw the pitch pipe out of her desk.

One thing about Mrs. Foster that Laura did not like was the fact that everybody had to sing in her class. Many teachers believed in having a group of children known as listeners, but not Mrs. Foster. In order to be a listener, you simply had to be a terrible singer, to which category Laura felt she belonged. Mrs. Foster said that everybody could sing, and that in her class nobody listened.

" 'John Peel,' " suggested Mrs. Foster.

She blew a note in the pitch pipe, tapped her foot once, waved her hand, and off they went.

Do you ken John Peel
By the break of day?

Do you ken John Peel
In his coat so gay?
Do you ken John Peel
When he's far, far away
With his hounds and his horn
In the morning?


Aunt Minnie left right after they finished
singing "John Peel," but Mrs. Kahn and Mrs.
Rosenkranz remained through "Oh, Susanna"
and "Home on the Range." Laura knew
that Aunt Minnie was going to Amy's classroom now. What would Mrs. Malucci say?
she wondered, stiffening a little. Amy certainly was afraid of her. Laura just wished
she was old enough to tell her off, like Mama
would if she had been able to come. Like
Mama did to Miss Potter. Laura frowned and
ran her teeth around her braces. What was
Mama thinking, sitting there in the wheel
chair? What would *she* think if she had to sit
in a wheel chair and have somebody else go
and talk to her children's teachers during
Open School Week?

All through the rest of the day, grownups
continued to arrive. Some wore proud, happy
looks on their faces after talking with Mrs.
Foster; others looked throughtful; a few cast
menacing looks at their children. It was gra-

tifying for Laura to note how many times Mrs. Foster kept calling on her, along with Marjorie Kahn and Jack Lazarus. Not that she meant to count or anything, but she *had* been called on the most — eight times to seven for Marjorie and seven for Jack. She had no worries about what Mrs. Foster had said to Aunt Minnie.

After dismissal, Laura hurried down the stairs. She would dash home, hear what Aunt Minnie had to say, and then get over to the park as quickly as she could. Gloria Fernbach and Helen Franklin had promised her that they would be biking this afternoon.

Amy and Cynthia were standing in the schoolyard, talking.

"I'm not going home," Cynthia was saying. "Did you see the way my mother looked at me? I think I'll go home with you."

"No," Amy said glumly. "I don't think it'll be so good at my house either."

"Maybe we both should go to Annette's house," Cynthia suggested. "Her mother didn't come."

"No. What's the sense of waiting?" said Amy. "I'm going home."

"Well, I can wait," Cynthia said. "I'm just tired of always getting smacked during Open School Week. Bye." She darted off.

"Well?" Laura asked, taking Amy's arm. From the drift of the conversation that had just taken place, she had a pretty good idea of what had happened.

Amy shook her head miserably. "She talked to Aunt Minnie outside in the hall. I couldn't hear anything."

Laura's arm crept comfortingly around her sister's shoulder. What could anybody say after that? Silently the girls headed toward home. This Mrs. Malucci was really a monster, Laura reflected. All right, granted Amy was no brain — but she wasn't a dope either. Plenty of kids in her class were dumber than she was — like Cynthia, for instance. Why should Mrs. Malucci pick on her so much? Laura swelled with indignation. Something had to be done. If only Mama could come. But no — Mama was helpless in the wheel chair, and mustn't hear anything disagreeable. "Poor Amy," Laura thought, and then suddenly "Poor Mama."

"You go ahead. I'll come in a minute," Amy said when they reached their stoop. Her lower lip began to tremble.

"I'll think of something," Laura said desperately. "Tomorrow I'll go and talk to her. I'll tell her what I think."

Amy looked at her hopelessly. "She won't

listen to you," she said miserably. "There's nothing we can do. Just don't tell Mama."

"I won't," Laura promised. She walked slowly through the door and up the stairs. "Poor Mama," she thought again. "Thank goodness she doesn't know."

# Amy and Laura

Mama and Aunt Minnie were sitting in the living room when Laura opened the door.

"Laura!" Aunt Minnie called.

"Uh huh." Laura closed the door and walked thoughtfully into the room. Mama was sitting in the wheel chair, and she smiled at Laura and said, "What a lovely report Mrs. Foster gave Aunt Minnie. I'm so pleased with you, Laura."

Her face had such a familiar, proud look on it that Laura felt confused. All those other Open School Weeks (except for one), she had rushed home from school, hurried into the house, and dashed straight into Mama's lap, where she could hide her embarrassed face against Mama's shoulder and listen to all the good things her teacher had said about her.

But today her feet carried her over to the couch, and she sat down and murmured, "I'm glad."

"She really thinks you're the greatest," Aunt Minnie said, laughing and began telling

Laura all the delightful things Mrs. Foster had said about her.

Laura listened, but instead of feeling good, she felt miserable. She felt even worse when Amy opened the door, and stood there with what was supposed to be a cheerful, unworried smile on her face. Amy was standing so straight and stiff that she looked as if something was wrong with her neck.

"Oh, there you are, Amy," Aunt Minnie said. "Wait until I tell you what your teacher said about you."

Amy's lower lip began trembling again, and Laura tried to catch Aunt Minnie's eye. Surely Aunt Minnie realized that whatever disagreeable remarks Mrs. Malucci had made must wait for later, outside on the stoop. Mama mustn't know. And she would just have to work out some way of dealing with Mrs. Malucci herself. But Mama said, "Amy, I never was so surprised in my whole life."

Amy's head dropped, and her lip trembled faster.

"I tell you," Aunt Minnie said, turning to Mama. "She just wouldn't let me go. Over and over again, the same thing. And all those mothers standing there waiting for her."

Amy was a silent bundle of misery in the doorway. Swiftly Laura rose from the couch, moved over to her sister, put a fierce arm around her, and said huskily, "She's a wonderful kid! Whatever anybody says!"

"Well, for a change," said Aunt Minnie, "it looks like everybody agrees."

And she began talking. And after a while Amy's lips stopped trembling, and her mouth looked like a pretzel without the part in the center. And then she was smiling. Everybody was smiling — except Laura. Because the things Mrs. Malucci had told Aunt Minnie in the hall were all *good!* Good wasn't even the word. Fantastic, really! Mrs. Malucci couldn't stop talking about what an amazing student Amy was. How original! How bright! How outstanding! It seemed incredible to her that Amy's previous teachers had not realized what a gold mine of scholarship lay behind Amy's curly head.

Yes, she did realize that if Amy had one fault, it was laziness; and that without proper encouragement, Amy did have a way of coasting along without effort. But Mrs. Malucci was happy to say that she was working very hard on that one fault of Amy's. She had given her more work than anybody else in the class, harder work, and each time Amy had proved that she could do it, and Mrs. Malucci felt pleasure that Amy was even eager for more work.

At this point Laura and Amy both wondered if perhaps Aunt Minnie wasn't just fabricating the whole story for Mama's benefit, and that later the real, dark truth would unfold on the stoop. But no, Aunt Minnie kept bubbling along, and all the pieces began slowly fitting together.

"But why in the hall?" Amy asked.

"I guess she felt the things she had to say about you were so good that if any of the other children heard them they might feel bad."

Amy's smile widened. "What about my 'My Best Friend' composition? Did she say anything about that?"

"Only that it was so good that she showed it to all the teachers on her floor."

Amy's smile looked like a crocodile's, and Laura felt scared. She knew that she should be sharing Amy's joy at this sudden reversal, but all she felt was fear. Amy was supposed to be her little sister — her pretty, brainless little sister, who needed her help desperately. Laura's mind was like one bursting bubble of confusion, and she struggled resentfully against all the horrible changes that were taking place. Not Amy! Not her too!

She took her arm off Amy's shoulder and cried, "I helped her with that composition!"

"You did not," Amy protested. "You just told me to say I couldn't say it, so I did. But I wrote it myself, and you didn't help."

"Well, other times I helped," Laura insisted. "How about all those other compositions I wrote for you, and the maps, and the . . ."

"No," Amy declared, looking at her reproachfully, "you didn't. Not this term. You're so busy all the time you never even get a chance to talk to me."

Mama smiled at both of them. "Well, it's a good thing she hasn't been helping you. Just look at how well you can do by yourself. None of us ever realized what a good student you could be, because you never really tried all by yourself." She looked seriously at Laura and said, "Sometimes when we think we're helping people by doing everything for them, we're really hurting them. Don't help Amy any more. She doesn't need any help."

"She does, she does!" Laura cried. "I've always helped her. She can't get along if I don't."

"I can too," Amy shouted, "and you're just jealous, that's all."

"Who's jealous?" Laura yelled.

"You are. You think you're the only smart one in the family, but you're not. I'm as good as you are, and I'm not going to let you pick on me any more."

"For someone who's supposed to be so smart, you're pretty stupid!" Laura shouted.

Amy reached up and scratched Laura's face, and Laura smacked Amy hard. In a minute they were rolling around on the floor. Laura pulled Amy's hair, and Amy sank her teeth into Laura's hand.

"Ouch!" Laura screamed.

"Girls!" Mama shouted.

"Stop it this minute!" yelled Aunt Minnie.

Two strong hands were pulling at them, shaking them apart. "Shame on you! Shame!" Mama said. She was leaning way down from her chair with a hand on each of them. "Get up this minute!" Her face was red and her eyes blazed.

"*She* started it!" Amy yelled, removing her teeth from Laura's hand and beginning to cry.

"*You* started it!" Laura cried.

"Just wait till I tell your father," said Aunt Minnie.

"Look at what you did!" Mama said angrily. "You knocked over the snake plant and you broke the pot. I just don't know what's the matter with the two of you, but let me tell you — " She stopped talking suddenly and said with surprise, "You know — I think this is the first time I've been angry — really angry — since I came home."

"And no wonder!" said Aunt Minnie.

"Don't tell Daddy," Amy sobbed. "He said not to fight, but it was all her fault. She started it, and he'll blame me. He'll talk to me on the stoop, and I can't stand it any more if he talks to me on the stoop."

"Be quiet!" Laura hissed. "Shut your big mouth!"

"What's that?" Mama said sharply.

"Don't mind her," Aunt Minnie said quickly. "You know the way she goes on and on about nothing."

"What does she mean, Harry will talk to her on the stoop?" Mama insisted.

Nobody said anything.

"I want to know what's happening here," Mama said, her eyes blazing again.

"Hannah," Aunt Minnie said gently, "we've all been trying, up until now," she paused and glanced reproachfully at the two girls, "to keep things peaceful and pleasant for you. Sometimes if Harry feels the girls aren't behaving, he just talks to them a little bit outside. He doesn't want you to worry about anything, that's all. Until you're better, I mean."

"We're not supposed to fight in front of you," Amy sobbed, "or make too much noise, or bother you, or — " the tears were rolling down her face, "be unhappy when you're around."

"No wonder it's been so quiet around here," Mama said, "so terribly quiet. You haven't wanted to upset me, and I haven't wanted to upset you, and all of us have been upset." She looked down at the brace on her leg. "I don't like this brace, and I don't like sitting in a wheel chair." Her voice was trembling. "Just sitting and not doing anything all day long, and not knowing what's happening in my own house."

Aunt Minnie and the girls looked at each other in horror. This was the first time they had heard Mama complain since she came home from the hospital.

"Mama," Laura said helplessly, "what can we do?"

"Do?" Mama repeated, looking up at her. Amy was still sobbing, and Mama shook her head, reached out, and pulled Amy over to her. Amy crumpled into her lap and lay there crying comfortably against her shoulder. "I guess you've done it," Mama said, stroking Amy's head. "You had that fight, and now I really know I'm home. And from now on it's going to be different. I'm not going to sit and be waited on like an invalid. If anything's wrong, I want to know about it; and if you two feel like fighting, go right ahead and fight. Your father doesn't have to talk to you on the stoop, because you'll hear from me soon enough if I don't like how you're behaving."

"We were only trying to do the best for you," Aunt Minnie said sadly.

"I know, I know, Minnie," Mama said gently. "You've been wonderful, but it's like with Amy here. A person has to do for himself. Certain things nobody can do for him."

She looked up at the drapes, and Laura held her breath because she knew what was going to happen next. Maybe nobody else knew, but she did. Mama hated those drapes, and somehow Laura realized that Mama's recovery and those drapes were tied up together.

"Minnie," Mama said softly, "those drapes now . . ."

"Yes, I know," sighed Aunt Minnie. All the worry and tension faded from her face. She smiled complacently and looked up at them. "They sort of make you forget your troubles, don't they? I feel good every time I look at them."

Laura wanted to put both fingers in her ears to shut out the words that Mama would speak. In spite of the many times that she and Aunt Minnie had not agreed on various points, she could not bear to see her hurt, as she was sure to be now.

But Mama never finished what she was going to say. She looked at Aunt Minnie, back at the drapes, frowned, stroked Amy's hair again, and her eyes settled on the couch.

"I think," she said slowly, "that I'd like to make some new slip covers for the couch and chair."

"I thought of that too," Aunt Minnie said enthusiastically, "but there wasn't time before you came home, and it would have cost too much anyway to use the same material."

"No, no, not the same material!" Mama said quickly. "Yes, that *would* be too expensive. But maybe if Harry can take me over to Drexler's this weekend, I could pick out some inexpensive material. Maybe something gray for the couch and a nice quiet print for the chair. Yes!" Her face wrinkled thoughtfully. "Of course. That would do it. Why didn't I think of it before?"

She began looking around the room again, as if she were seeing it for the first time. "We could even turn the rug. I think if we changed it around, that worn spot would be hidden by the chair."

Aunt Minnie nodded unsuspectingly, and Laura let her breath out slowly. Trust Mama to find another way. There always was another way, but few people had the grace and wisdom to find it as Mama had. She looked at the woman in the wheel chair with recognition. It *was* Mama. It had always been Mama, but she, Laura, had been so selfish, so preoccupied with her own feelings, that she had not seen it.

She hurried over to Mama, grabbed her hand, and said, "Mama, if you don't want me to go biking, I won't any more." It was the only thing she could think of at that moment to make up to Mama for all those selfish, painful weeks that had gone before.

Mama pressed Laura's hand. "What a good girl you are!" she said gently. And Laura shook her head violently. "No, no, I'm not. I've been mean and selfish, but I won't any more, and I'll never ride a bike again as long as I live. I'll come home every day and help you, and do whatever you want me to. I'll — "

"No, darling," Mama said firmly. "I don't want you to stay home every day. And you won't have to help me — and that goes for all of you — because I want to do things by myself."

She looked at Laura as if she were seeing her for the first time too — like the couch and the chair. "You keep right on biking. Daddy is right — it's good for you. I have to

169

remember that you're a big girl now." She sighed. "I have to learn that I can't protect you either."

Then Laura was sitting in Mama's lap too, along with Amy, and Mama was hugging both of them.

"Get up, both of you!" Aunt Minnie yelled. "What's the matter with you?" But she didn't sound really angry.

So the girls jumped up, and Mama said, "You both look like Mary Sugarbowl. Go wash up, and we'll have some cocoa."

"I'll make it," Aunt Minnie said.

"No, let me," Mama insisted, rolling her wheel chair down the long hall to the kitchen.

Laura followed Amy into the bathroom and watched her as she washed her face and buried it in her towel.

"Amy," she said.

No answer.

"Amy."

"Don't talk to me."

"Listen, Amy," Laura said generously. She felt so happy she could afford to be generous. "Go ahead and be smart. I don't really mind."

Amy's radiant face peered at her over the towel. "Isn't it wonderful?" she glowed. "I never really thought she liked me, and did you hear all the wonderful things she said to Aunt Minnie about me?"

"Mmm."

"That I'm the most original child she ever had?"

"Mmm."

"So bright?"

"Mmm."

"Nothing I can't do if I put my mind to it."

"Mmm."

"Outstanding in every way."

"She didn't say *that*."

"No?" Amy blinked thoughtfully. "I thought she did."

"She didn't."

"She did so."

"She did not."

"*She did!*" Amy threw the towel on the clothes hamper and shouted, "I don't want to talk to you as long as I live!" She hurried out of the room, slamming the door behind her.

"Brat!" Laura thought. "By tomorrow she'll be running after me to help her with her work. But I won't any more. I just won't. She'll beg me, and cry and scream, but I'll say, 'Go ahead. You want to be smart — go ahead and be smart — by yourself.' "

Briskly she washed her face and rubbed it against the prickly towel. Mama was making cocoa in the kitchen, and Laura hoped she was making a lot. She hung up the towel and inspected her face in the mirror. Her hair was a mess. She picked up her brush and began brushing it. How long it had grown! She hadn't had a haircut in ages. She worked away at it, and noted with satisfaction that it was down to her shoulders now and looked shinier than when she wore it short. Maybe she should let it grow longer and wear it hanging down her back. She put down the brush, drew a little closer to the mirror, and studied her teeth, and then her nose and her eyes and her forehead. The same as ever — and yet . . . Why not? Miracles did happen, and if Amy could be smart, why couldn't she be — ? She laughed and shut her eyes in embarrassment at the ridiculous thought that was flooding her mind.

"Mama!" she shouted, hurrying out of the room, "Mama! Give me something to eat. I'm starving."